T0207906

Love

Comes Through Time

KN James

authorHOUSE®

AuthorHouse™
1663 Liberty Drive
Bloomington, IN 47403
www.authorhouse.com
Phone: 1 (800) 839-8640

Published by AuthorHouse 01/13/2016

ISBN: 978-1-5049-7087-7 (sc)
ISBN: 978-1-5049-7086-0 (e)

Print information available on the last page.

Chapter 1

May 31, 1860 Morning

Dear Diary,

    I'm sitting at my desk looking out the window. Indianapolis is an active town this morning. We too are occupied as well, along with mama trying to cook and the house maids cleaning. Our family and the Kent family are expecting company. Well, I need to go now; I probably should see whether mama will need my help.

    Love Katherine

…

    I lied about helping mama. After writing that last sentence I put my writing utensil down and closed the book. I sat there for a few minutes staring out the window. I stood up quickly from my chair, which afterwards fell back behind me to close the curtains to the window. Then I went to the next window to do the same. It got dark quick. I pulled the chair right-side up, and then started walking around the room. I spent a lot of time up, here doing whatever there is to do here. I like to stay up here just to get away from my parents. I then lay down on my bed.

I heard a knock upon my door; it scared me.

"Miss, are you up?" called out one of the maids.

"E-yes I'm up," I hesitated.

"Well, your mother would like to see you." I had no comment to that. I waited a minute for the maid to leave me before I headed downstairs. I got up and started walking towards the door, down the hallway, down the stairs, and into the kitchen where my mother was.

"Oh good your dress," she said looking at me as she grabbed the pan of biscuits out of the oven.

"You wanted to see me?" I asked.

"Yes for two reasons. One, is what was that noise I heard up stairs and two is its quarter past eight, and we need to get breakfast out of the way before our guest arrives," she said placing the biscuits in a basket and moving them to the dining room.

"That nose was my chair falling," I said. I and the maids were caring the dishes into the dining room.

"I'll need your help in the kitchen after breakfast. You and I are going to cook."

"But mama you don't know how to cook, and you won't tell me the names of our guest. I'm lost right now." She said nothing after that last comment. She then left the dining room to go get father, I sat down to wait for them. We all began to eat in silence.

Do all rich families' mamas cook or just mine? I'm proud of her for trying. Father doesn't appreciate it. Father was born in Georgia. His father owned a plantation along with slaves. Mama is from here in Indianapolis. I look up from my plate; father was staring at me. He smiled then I smiled back. He usually never smiles. I took a bite out of my biscuit. Where was I, oh yes about my parent's. Both of my grandparents were all friends when they were younger. They had it plan out for my mother and father to get married. Mama and father got married and had me end of story.

Katherine!

Katherine!

I kept on hearing my name called out louder and louder. "Katherine," I jumped. Mama was standing next to me saying my name. "Sorry yes?"

"You're going to help me in the kitchen," she said then left. "Now!" she yelled across the hall. I stood up quickly and walked over towards her.

"What is it that you want me to do?" I asked because I had no clue on what to do.

"Make bread." She subjected. I wasn't that good along with the recipe; I still couldn't figure it out. I had to have one of our maids who makes our meals help me. My mother wasn't doing to well herself. I love my parents, but they have other people do their work for them. And it's been like that for years. Hours have gone by for us, the time showing three o'clock and the Kent family just arrived. Elizabeth their daughter came up to my room with me to talk. I realized that our dresses were the same but different color. She wore a dark-red dress, and I had on a dark blue. We both don't like to dress all rich. We hate that we have lots of money, and most people don't. Our mother's hate that we have the choice to dress poorly, and yet they aren't stopping us.

Elizabeth sat on my extra chair as I sat at the one that belongs to my desk. However, before I sat down I opened the curtains to let the light shine through.

"I feel all lost?" I said.

"Yes I too," she answered.

"I tried my best to have my mother tell me the names of our guest, but she won't tell me," I said waving my arm around.

"And I asked the same as well," she said.

We were up in my room for a good 45 minutes. That's the longest time that mine and Elizabeth's parents let us stay up there. Our parents always want us to talk downstairs just so they can eavesdrop on our conversations. However, this time I think they were too busy to notice.

There was a knock upon my door. I opened it up and to see one of our house maids standing there. It was the one from earlier.

"Sorry to bother you miss but your parents want you two girls to be downstairs. Supper will be done shortly," she said then left. The maids aren't supposed to talk to us much because they have to do their work, and my parents made it a rule. However, I let them talk to me even if it gets me in trouble.

"Thank you!" I yelled across the hall after that turned around quickly to look at Elizabeth. We later left the room and started walking down the hallway.

"You don't suppose that our mystery guests are here yet do you?" Elizabeth asked as we were making the turn on the staircase going down.

"I'm not sure," I said. Our parents were all in the study room. All the food was already on the table ready to be eaten. Elizabeth and I had no reason to go in the other room; instead, we sat down and waited until the others to join.

They came one by one into the dining room, both mama's and fathers.

"Well let's begin to eat now. I believe our guests were maybe running a little late, which is alright," said father. We were getting ready to eat before we heard a knock upon the door. We were all looking towards the door waiting for one of the maids to answer it. She opened the door slowly, "Sir?" she asked turning her head to father. Father got up and walked over to the door then smiled big.

He looked back at us and said," Our guests are here." He invited them in. Two men came through the door and took off their hats. Elizabeth's father got up then our mama's.

Elizabeth and I stayed seated. Then mama gave me a look. It was a look telling us to get up. I got up and so did Elizabeth. She would only do something if I do it, and I'm the same at her house as well. Everyone was moving into the study room for greeting and a quick conversation.

"Our supper will get cold," I whispered to Elizabeth as she nods back. So I guess our supper wasn't important.

"Girls these are our friends Dan and his brother David," said father putting his hands on the backs of the two men. "They'll be staying with us for a while," he added. There was a long pause until Mrs. Kent said, "Well our supper is getting cold. We can talk while we're eating."

"Right this way gentleman," said mama as she was leading the way to the supper table.

The brothers were classy men, born and raised on wealth. They lived on a plantation down south together. I was disgusted of the word *plantation* because they have slaves. Yes, we have maids and I'm disgusted by that as well. The grownups were the ones that were laughing. Elizabeth and I simply thought a few things were funny. Both of us didn't talk or should I say didn't have time. There were too many questions rolling off the table.

So after supper we all migrated to the study room again, but this time we stayed. During supper, the talks were, how are you, and what's the weather like down there? No. After supper, we get to the serious questions *while drinking or sipping tea.*

"So which one is the oldest?" Mrs. Kent asked. "I am," said Dan or is that David; I only got their names once. One has a long mustache, and the other one has a beard that was a little shorter than fathers.

"I'm 32 and my brother David will be 31 in two weeks ma'am," I had it right.

"What's on your mind honey," Mama asked.

"Just daydreaming, mama," and I was.

"Women aren't supposed to daydream," said father.

"I agree sir. No wife of mine will be doing that soon," said... Dan. No David. It was David; he's the one with the long mustache. And what was he saying about, 'Wife of mine.' I wonder what's going on in Elizabeth's mind? I looked up to see her face; I was seated upon the chair, and Elizabeth was sitting on the arm rest.

"Wife," I spook up while they all were in conversation. One by one they were all looking at me.

"Yes," father hesitated with a laugh. "What," I whispered to myself. Mama was looking at me the most with those sad eyes as the other five all had a smirk on their face. Did I say something?

"The proposals were to be in two weeks but now would be good," said father.

"Elizabeth, Katherine. Dan and David are to be your husband's!" Mr. Kent said with joy.

"This calls for a good bottle of champagne!" Dan yelled. Father, Mr. Kent, and Mrs. Kent were clapping with joy. I looked at Elizabeth, who looked at me when I turned my head to see mama. She looked to be not in a cheering mod. I stood up saying, "No."

Everybody is staring at me. Both brothers looked confused like our parents had talked to them about the arrange marriages.

"No," father asked angrily. "No," I said again.

"Young lady," his voice was low and deep as I entrapped him. "You can say young lady to me all you want but no. You expect us to fall in love now, right now? We're seventeen, father." I kept on going before they could even start.

"Y'all don't know what love is," I said. "But," father again. "Love isn't saying you're going to get married on your parent's watch, hell no! You can't expect us to shack hands and fall in love; it doesn't work like that."

"But you girls didn't shake hands," Mrs. Kent laughed with a high pitch squeal thinking; she knows everything. I gave her an ugly look.

"This isn't love," Elizabeth said standing up. "Elizabeth," her mother and father yelled at the same time. "Mother, father no," she added.

"Love is two people getting to know one another and seeing them repeatedly," I explained.

"That's just friends," said David which I think he was going to be *my* husband; I'm only guessing.

"If you had any you would understand," Elizabeth yelled.

"I'm stopping the arrange marriages," and those were my final words.

I took Elizabeth by the arm, and we ran out of the study room, down the hall, and up to my room. Once there I closed my door with a chair. We had anger written all over our faces. A few moments of silence were between us. We heard yelling from downstairs.

"Katherine it's your mother. It pleases me if you let me in."

"Katherine no," Elizabeth whispered. "I have to," I whispered back barley hearing myself. I opened the door slowly only trying to see if it was mama, and it was. She came in and moved the chair back in front of the door where I had it at.

She came and hugged me. She was warm.

"Mama, do we have to marry those men?"

"Ma…"

"No Katherine," she cried still hugging me. I never want her to let go. And after a few seconds, we all calmed down.

Chapter 2

All three of us girls were sitting on the bed. Probably thinking, I was thinking but nothing came to mind. There was still yelling going on downstairs. The only thought that was in my mind was the men and us. If I go, I would be trapped. No one would hear me screaming.

"Run," mama said. Elizabeth and I looked at her. She was in the middle of us on the bed.

"What," I said.

"Run. Run off. Pack your clothes and *run far,*" she sounded scared. I was scared.

"Where," I asked.

"I'm not sure?" she answered.

"And what about me," Elizabeth asked to frighten.

"Yes my dear you as well," mama whispered with her eyes closed. She got up and grabbed my trunk from under the bed. She was already packing for me. She then went through my chest and started grabbing my dresses.

She was pulling them out nervously fast. Her hands were shaking; I have never seen her like this before. I leaned over on my side to touch her hand.

"Mama why are you helping us," I asked. She stopped what she was doing, and then looked up at me with a sad gentle stare.

"I wish I could have run!" She said with every word panicking. I looked at her confused all day I've been confused. She went on, "I love your father very much, and you know that, Katherine,"

"Yes mama," I answered.

"I do. I love him!" she cried.

"Yes mama I know," I answered again.

"I didn't want to marry him when we were younger. I was already seeing someone secretly," she tried hard to calm herself by moving her left hand over her mouth. We then both stood up hugging.

"I was too late to say something, anything to my parents. The night before the wedding I finally got the nerve to tell my one love what was going to happen to us, *especially me.*"

"Katherine you know we're wealthy?"

"Yes mama," she didn't say anything for a few seconds.

"He was poor," she whispered. I looked deep into those frighten brown eyes.

"Poor mama I'm shocked," I raised my voice to a louder sound. Mama quickly covered my mouth and shushed me.

"Not so loud," she whispered.

"And you never told father anything," I asked.

"No he would have beaten me," she said looking at the floor. I guess we were talking for a while because I saw Elizabeth waving us down for her to say something.

"Excuse me but weren't we going to talk about an escape plan," Elizabeth asked.

"Yes!" mama said. Mama finished packing my trunk. I was packing my diary and with whatever money I had been lying around. Mama told me she was going into her room to get some more money. She was trying hard not to make any noise while she was doing her task.

"Ok I'm ready," I say.

"I see but I'm not. How are we to get to my house?" Elizabeth asked.

"Girls we can take the stairs outside that lead to both of our back yards."

"Mamas right let's go." And we stared heading out of my room and quietly down the hallway, and to the right of us was the door to the outside stairs.

Once when we got to the ground, we had forgotten about the fines.

"Oh no I forgot about the fines," mama panicked.

"Don't worry there's a few boards that are loose that we can slide right through," Elizabeth said while moving a few boards out of the way. When we got to the back yard of Elizabeth's house, we didn't know if Elizabeth's parents were home yet. So we had Elizabeth go first to open the back door to the kitchen.

"Why miss Elizabeth. What are you doing back so early?" It must be one of her house hold maids. They only have a few less than we do.

"Are my parent's home?" she asked.

"No I thought they were with you?" Elizabeth turned around and said, "They're still at your house and will probably be home soon we should be quick." We walked past the one maid who had a confused smile on her face.

"Miss Elizabeth what is this all about?" The same maid asked.

"Mama set my things down here and go help Elizabeth pack. I'll explain things to her," I said. Mama set my trunk down and she, and Elizabeth ran to find the stairs.

"What is going on here?" she asked. I have a lot of explaining to do or maybe not.

"Elizabeth and I are running away from what our parents want our lives to be," is that what you want to here?

"Why are you running away from a problem dreary?" Why so many questions?

"I think you would if you were set up for an arraign marriage," she said nothing after that. Instead, she smiled and turned around and was looking at a plate of bread.

"You're going to tell them aren't you," I asked.

"No dreary."

"Thank you but why not," I was confused. Why not tell on us? She was still looking at the bread.

There was a window there in the kitchen. I was looking out of it to see if Elizabeth's parents were coming back. I haven't seen them yet so that was good. Although if we were gone for a while what would they be doing still at my house, probably drinking?

She started slicing the bread and then putting a few in a basket. She hands it the basket of sliced bread over to me and left the kitchen. She never answered my one question. And I didn't want to take the bread, so I left it. I was starting to get worried about mama and Elizabeth. Wait there they are coming down the stairs.

"Okay we need to go now," I said. Elizabeth then sat down at the desk in the hallway.

"Elizabeth what are you doing?" I asked she was writing something.

"I'm writing a good bye letter to my parents. Because I know that I'll never see them again,"

"Well will you please make it quick," we had no time to waste. I wanted to leave this place forever. So now she was finished. We then left the house. Mama couldn't come with us because of father even though it involved her to be beaten by him. However, she is doing it for our safety.

Mama first hugged Elizabeth then me. "I want you two to head east. I'll tell your father that you were heading west" she whispered. "Thank you," I whispered into her ear.

"Be safe," she cried. "I love you," a tear was coming down from the side of my cheek as we then started heading east into the evening.

"I just hope we will find an Inn to sleep at," I said. Elizabeth was not up to talk as we were walking.

"I just don't see why we had to leave," she said. We were only a few houses down the street in eye contact if Elizabeth's parents came out. Mama was still standing there. I stopped to face Elizabeth and said, "Elizabeth we need to leave. We have to leave for the good of it!" I yelled and then said, "Money and no love or love and no money." It was to give her time to think about it and myself.

She was fed up with it with all the commotion. I could tell that she was done with it; however, I wasn't going to let her leave and throw away her life just for nothing but a big bed to sleep in at night, and a few kids whom she would love but not him.

I remember that there was an Inn just a few blocks away from here. I hope for now that they have a room for us. It's a small Inn and can fill up quick to dinner time for travelers. So now we got to the Inn and were waiting for someone to check us in. There was an elderly grandfather clock in the lobby saying eight thirty-four pm occurred. There was an old man at the front desk reading a book. He looked like he was about to pass out and fell asleep. He was really into his book because when Elizabeth, and I walked up to the desk; he didn't look at us. So I made a cough sound to get his attention.

"May I help you?" he asked tiered and bored.

"Yes we would like a room just for tonight," I said. He got out the papers for me to sign and a key.

"You're lucky we only have one room available for now," he said. I got out the money to pay him as he handed me the key. "Room two," he said in a boring tone. We then grabbed our trunks and headed up the stairs to our room. There were one bed, one window, one desk, and two chairs one at the desk and the other by the window. What we did first was moved our trunks onto the bed and went our separate ways with our own diaries. I took the desk while Elizabeth went to the window to write.

May 31 still 1860 Night

Dear Diary,

A lot has happened to me today since the last time I wrote. Elizabeth and I are at the Inn just a few blocks down from our houses. We are running away from our parents. Besides mama, father and Elizabeth's parents wants us two to get married to two strangers. A guy named Dan and his brother David. They are two wealthy men. So that is why we are running away. We don't know where we are going. Mama said for us to head east as she tells father we were going to head west. I am scared for what is to come for us tomorrow.

I believe Elizabeth is mad at me for yelling at her earlier. At first, she was all with mama and I about the running away plan but then got all fed up with it. Right now, she is sitting on the chair next to the window writing in her diary. I just hope for the best for tomorrow. Now I need to count how much money we have left. When I paid I didn't have time to see how much money mama gave me.

We had no time to go to the bank to get more money so what we have will have to last us for a while. Tomorrow we must leave early and only walk to the next town because I don't want to spend our money on anything but a room for the night and what food we can buy. I am going to sleep now maybe I'll write tomorrow I'm not sure.

Love Katherine

...

I looked over to Elizabeth's way she was still writing. I closed my book to put it away for the night. What I need now is sleep. I'm just going to sleep in what I have on, I really don't care if it's my evening dress. I haven't looked at what mama packed me as I think about it as I'm moving my trunk off of the bed. As I pull the blankets down, I can see that the bed was dirty with stains, I'm not used to that, but I'm going to have to for now on.

Mama slid our money into my bag with my diary. I counted forty eight to be my total. For my family being rich that sure isn't enough money for two people for who knows how long until we can find a permanent place to live. However, we didn't have time to go to the bank and deposit some money out. I put back the money into my bag and crawled into bed. Elizabeth was just now finishing up with her writing. And to finish for the night while falling to sleep, I just pray for the best for tomorrow.

Chapter 3

Am I awake yet no asleep yes? I don't want to get up, but I have to because I heard Elizabeth get up. So I got up. I woke up to find an empty room. I must have fallen back to sleep then. Elizabeth must be down stairs to the restaurant checking things out; I hope. I didn't change only brushed my hair; I slept in what I had on yesterday. Her things were still in the room so that was a good sign. Now I'm hungry, so I think I'll go check things out down stairs.

Once when I reached the restaurant, I saw Elizabeth setting at a table with a cup of coffee. She didn't change either. I walked over toward her way and said, "Is this seat taken?"

"No sit," she said softly. I waited a few seconds to say something anything.

"Do we have to pay for the meals?" I asked hoping she would answer me.

"No since we paid for a room, we get the meals included. I was waiting for you to get up, so we can eat together," she said sipping her coffee.

"Well I'm starving let's order something," I said feeling all good inside because she said that she was waiting on me to get up.

She and I grabbed the two menus to look at what they have.

"You know what on second thought I can wait until dinner to eat. I would feel a little better once when we get out of the city," I said.

"Ok I can wait as well. Do you want to finish the rest of my coffee? I'm done drinking it?" she asked.

"Sure."

Now I can see why she was done with it. It wasn't even that good, but I drank it all of what was left of it. We then left the restaurant dining room to go back up to our room to grab our trunks.

"So last night I could tell that you were mad at me Elizabeth," I said to her as we walked into our room. She looked back at me.

"Yes I was a little mad, but I forgive you."

"You do?" I was confused. Why does she forgive me?

"When I was down in the restaurant at the table by myself, I was thinking what today would be like if we didn't leave home?" She was looking at me all ready to leave. I smiled at her ready to leave as well.

"I see," I said quietly.

"I counted our money of what we have left."

"Oh and how much is there?" she asked. I know she isn't going to like my answer but, "Forty eight."

"Oh now I see why you were asking about the meals?" she answered. I shook my head yes and smiled.

"Are you ready? I want to be at the next town by tonight if that's possible."

"Yes," she said and we left.

The streets were busy this morning again like always. Elizabeth and I were walking until I stopped to faces her to say, "You know we are going to have to walk the whole time until we get to the next town?"

"I understand," she replied back with a calm voice. I understand that it's going to be a long walk. Plus we have to carry our luggage. We then started walking again.

. . .

I bet hours have gone by. We were so tired of walking and getting sweaty. At least, we were out of the city. We weren't in the need to walk fast or to feel like we had to be in the next town by sundown. We were going at our own past which I really liked because we had more time to bond.

The only time we would take breaks would be when we are next to a river or stream. We just had a break to rest our legs and arms from caring our luggage and to get a drink from the cool water.

I never traveled much out of the city to see the beauty of the country. However, I think Elizabeth, and I were truly amazed by how beautiful the country side honestly is.

"There," Elizabeth yelled pointing her left hand out. We saw a few buildings so it must be the next town, but I never saw a sign, maybe I missed it.

"I hope they have a restaurant or something," I said. I believe the time should be at least four o'clock to five o'clock. I forgot to see what time we left the Inn. Time is everything to us now. We need to watch out for the time because what if father didn't go west like mama said we were going and started heading east on the same road that we are traveling on. I'm so worried and hungry. Maybe I should have brought that basket of sliced bread with us, but I wasn't thinking clearly.

Finally, we arrive in the town with no signs of what the name is. It was a small town but growing. There was a new building being built. I haven't seen an Inn, hotel or a restaurant. However, we haven't walked all the way through the streets.

"Elizabeth," I called her name to get her attention. She looked back at me saying, "Yes."

"Umm..." I hesitated; I had no energy to speak, and I know she didn't either.

"Can we take a break here my feet are getting tired."

"Sure mine as well." And we sat down on the wooden porch in front of what looks to be a general store. We just sat there on the side walk looking at the people of the city walking by. I hate how it's been hour's scents we've eaten from last night.

"Well," I said.

"Well," she said. I don't know what to say or do.

"The court house..." she murmured. I wasn't sure on what she said after the house honestly. It all became faint to hear, and then she left me.

"I'll be right back," she yelled from the middle of the street. I didn't say anything to her. So I got up grabbed our things, or so I thought I did and started walking towards her. I was out in the middle of the road with her out of sight.

I stood there looking for her until I started hearing a nose of rumble. I looked straight ahead of me and saw the people running out of the way, for some reason? Then I glanced back behind me and saw a wagon charging as fast as it can. I started to run but then tripped. Dirt was in my mouth and all over me. When I saw the wagon coming closer I tried to get up but then failed. I was not quick enough.

Until then, I felt someone grabbing my arm and my waist pulling me to the side walk. When we fell I fell on top of *him* just realizing that it was a young man who saved me. "Ethan," It was a name I heard called out and the only one. I had my eyes closed the whole time until when we fell upon the ground. Then I opened them. It was chest to chest between the both of us with his back to the ground and mine facing the air. We were both breathing really hard until he said, "Are you alright?"

I'm guessing this is the same man who was yelling; the one name came running up knelling. He came to the ground yelling at the young man who saved me. We were still on the ground. I didn't look up yet at the other man to see his face only the one that I am laying on top of.

"Ethan what in the world, were you thinking?" he asked.

"Be quiet Eric," he yelled facing his head to the other man and then back to face me. I had my mouth open for no reason.

"Once more are you alright?" he asked another time.

"Yes I'm okay," I said looking at him not moving. I really got a good glimpse of him now. He had a beautiful face with short brown hair, brown eyes and with freckles.

"Are you sure that you're okay? No bumps or bruises, scraps nor scratches, is the world spinning, you're head hurting?" he made it sound all funny.

"No I, I think I'm fine," I answered him. I finally got off of him well moved to sit my butt onto the ground. With it being close to sundown, the sun was making it hard for me to see the other man. Then there was a hand waiting for me to grab to help me up. I took a grip to it as the other person helped me.

A few of the town's people came running up to us talking among them. I felt a hand touching the middle of my back. I must have looked overwhelming. Where's Elizabeth at? Was it the young man's hand touching my back? The one man was talking to the other people to leave, and that they have things covered with me. As the crowed of people were leaving I saw what looks to be the sheriff of the town walking up to us.

"Is she okay?" he asked but to them instead. He looked at me and back to the two men and said, "We tried to catch him, but he was too far away for us. I hope the best for you miss." Elizabeth was still gone; I'm getting worried about her.

The one hand moved away from my back. I turned to facing the two young men. Wait twins?

"Miss, can you tell me your name?" The brown headed asked.

"Katherine, Katherine Stone," I answered then saying, "And yours please?" "Lee, Ethan Lee, and this here is my brother Eric," he said pointing to his hand to his right side where his brother was standing.

"How do you do ma'am," he said almost like a cowboy would say.

"Twins I assume?" I asked squinting my eyes. It was hard for me to see them; I could only make out two broad figures.

"Yes," Ethan hesitated while the two brothers moved so that I could see them better. Now Ethan has brown hair and eyes with freckles. Eric's hair was a few more inches longer and blond with blue eyes and with a little fewer freckles.

"There you are Katherine; I was looking for you," and theirs Elizabeth.

"Where did you go?" I asked.

"I went into the courthouse. I told you this. I was…" she started.

"Well hello there Miss," Eric interrupted her while stepping past Ethan and closer to her.

"Hello," she sounded confused on what was going on. In the circle of us young folks I was facing Ethan, on his right was Eric, who was on my left. Eric was facing Elizabeth, who was on my right and Ethan on her right.

"My names Eric," he said.

"Elizabeth. Katherine!" yeah she says her name all calm but mine, she yelled it. I could see that Eric was about to say something ells until Elizabeth started to say something to me.

"Why are you covered with dirt?" she asked while puling part of my skirt. I looked at her with part of my mouth open. I was thinking of what to tell her, but I was a little scared of what to say.

"I saved her life," Ethan said. He just did the hardest thing for me, telling the truth besides saving me. She looked at me confused yet again.

"Are you okay?" she said all concerned. She next moved her arm to hold me close after that said, "What happened?"

"She was out in the middle of the road, and a crazy man with his wagon was approaching her. If I wasn't there to push her, and myself out of the way she wouldn't be standing here right now." He told it better than I would. Her face was a mixture of madness and confused.

"Well thank you and you are?"

"Ethan and this is my twin brother whom you've already met," he said. Eric left us, but I saw him walking toward our luggage. He was bringing us our things.

"I've never seen you girls around here before are you new or just passing through?" Ethan asked.

"We were just passing through, but the man from the courthouse was telling me that the Inn in town was expensive, and we don't have much money left and have a clue to where we're going?" Elizabeth said. Eric lends over close to Ethan's ear while the two brothers were staring at us.

"Would you girls like to stay the night with us and our family? There's no cost and you'll get a good meal," Ethan asked. Elizabeth and I exchange looks.

"Yes we would love to come, but it won't be too much for you. I mean you just saved my life," I said.

"No. I'd rather keep on helping you and not myself," he added, but it didn't make since on what he was trying to say to us, and I was thinking he was thinking the same. The boys offered to carry our things for us. Elizabeth and I didn't mind. It was easy for our arms to rest for once. The boys lead the way to their wagon as we followed.

Chapter 4

We were just about out of town. Ethan was leading with one of my trunks and one of Elizabeth's bags. And Eric was at the back with one of Elizabeth's trunks and with one of my bags. I was third in line of this train of young kids. We then made it to their wagon. The boys had to move a few things in order to get our things and us to fit into the back. Ethan went on around front to untie the horses from their post. Eric was helping Elizabeth and me up into the wagon. I was first to get up in and like how Elizabeth is at times she rejected the help from Eric. The boys were sitting up front to drive. Ethan was sitting to the left, and Eric was sitting at the right. We then started to move. The ride home was about thirty to forty-five minutes long maybe? I was still so hungry.

"Let's hope Molly has supper ready for us this time," Ethan said to his brother.

"Who's Molly?" I asked.

"Is it your wife Eric," Elizabeth said very mean.

"No she's our mother," Ethan said. "There she is," he added.

"Your home," Elizabeth asked. Eric turned his head and smiled meaning yes, but Elizabeth ignored it. There were a few trees in the back yard with an outhouse. And behind the outhouse was what it looked to be a chicken coop. There was also a big barn off to the far left of the house. The barn and chicken coop were painted white and so was the house.

"What a beautiful land you have," I said. We pulled up into the drive and stopped. Then the boys jumped out to help us.

"We can leave your things in here and come and get them after supper," Ethan said. "That's fine with me," I said looking into those big brown eyes. I have to remember that Elizabeth, and I are on the run from our parents so there can't be any romance. Or so I guess?

"But we'll have to put the horses up though," Eric said. Each one was on one of the sides waiting to help us. They were such gentlemen I thought. Each one wanted to help us but its Elizabeth that is ruining the moment for me because of her meanest. Eric then ran in front of the wagon to put the horses up in the barn.

I was looking straight at the front of the house. The front door swung open, and it was a little girl who appeared in the middle of it. She was half in the house and half out with one leg swinging in front of her.

"Mama, mama the boys are back!" she cheered with a big smile on her face. She didn't look to be about ten to eleven years of age. Ethan left to help his brother and Elizabeth, and I didn't want to leave the wagon, so we stayed right next to it until they came back. The girl was looking inside the house. She had long wavy blond hair and was wearing a light-pink blouse with a brown skirt. She was very beautiful for her young age. I looked over my left to see if the boys were coming, and they were. Once when they made it to the wagon, the little girl was walking down the steps and ran towards Ethan cheering his name and gave him a big hug.

"Mama said you'd better get in a hurry and wash up, suppers about done," she said looking up at him. I saw Elizabeth gave a smile, and I was smiling as well.

"Ha," he laughed as he moved one of his arms around the back of her back. It looked to be in the same possession as it was when he had his arm behind my back.

"Girls this is one of our little sisters, Savanna," Ethan said.

"Shall we go inside," Eric smiled moving both arms and hands who were leading the way to the door. Ethan and Savanna lead the way with both arms locked in the back of their backs. Then it was Elizabeth and I with Eric in the back again. Somehow the odds just keep on coming to that.

Once inside, I saw there was a little boy setting the table in the other room. He was much younger than Savanna, who walked forward to help the little boy. Setting on one of the chairs was another girl about Savanna's age she was sewing. There was a woman in front of the fire place string in a pot. She was standing but was bent over. The fire place that she was at was in the room which we came in. I believe this is their kitchen.

When the lady stood she smiled confused and said, "Hello."

"Mama, these are our new friends we met today," Ethan said. The lady sure didn't look to be the boy's mother; she looked too young.

"Mama, this is Katherine," he said putting his hand on my back.

"And this is the beautiful Elizabeth," Eric said. He was touching her arm as he said that. I could see it on her face that she didn't like it but yet didn't want to say anything about it.

"Will you be staying for supper?" she asked wiping her hands with a white rag.

"Yes, they will be staying for supper, mama and the night if it's alright with you?" Ethan asked.

"Ethan may I have a word with you in the other room it will only take but just a moment," she asked reaching out with her arm. She looked back and said, "Come on in girls, make yourself at home." We were walking behind them. They turned left into another room, which looked to be her bedroom.

Eric ran to the little boy and picked him up. He cheered with joy. The other little girl was sitting at the end of the table. Elizabeth and I sat down close to her. Eric was sitting on the other side.

"What are your names again?" Savanna asked.

"Katherine and Elizabeth," I said pointing to me and Elizabeth.

"I'm Emma," the girl sewing said softly. She was stitching in a patch on a coat. I was the closest to be sitting next to her. I smiled back at her. Eric was tickling the little boy. He looked to be having fun then he stopped.

"This is Samuel one of my younger brothers," Eric said and *one* of his younger brothers? Are there more children here, there are already five kids? I was trying to listen to Ethan and *his mother*, but I couldn't from the crackling of the fire place and a few of the kids talking. Then I heard noses behind me. When I looked, I saw that there was a staircase. How did I miss that? Coming down from it was two girls and a boy who looked like the one Eric was tickling.

Three more children plus the five already downstairs is about eight kids.

"Mama never said we were having any guess tonight," said one of the girls from up stairs. Ethan came back now I'm glad I guess? The woman he was talking to came in behind him. She was patting down some rankles off her dark-blue skirt.

"Hello girls, I'm Molly Luke. I'm the mother of the house hold here," she said. I stood up with manners and looked her straight in her eyes with a pitiful smile.

"You girls are more than welcome to stay for supper and the night. Our home is always open," she said smiling.

"Now if you will excuse me, I have to check on supper," she said, then left to head into the kitchen. I wasn't done talking to her. Actually, I haven't gotten to say a word to her. She was already in the kitchen. I stared at Ethan then walked past him to go talk with his mother.

"Ma'am," I hesitated. She was bent over again string in the pot and tasting it. It was soup. She stood up and looked at me for a second then moved to the oven which I also didn't see when we came in the house.

"It's Molly," she said opening the oven and pulling out a pan of biscuits.

"Molly," I hesitated then laughed.

"Elizabeth and I thank you and your family very much for tonight," I said finally. She was placing the biscuits into a basket like how my mother doses it at home.

"But you see you don't know the whole story." Do I tell her the truth or say half of it and lie the rest of the way? She took the pot off of the fire to stop cooking and to cool down.

"Elizabeth's and my parents well *kicked* us out of our houses," there half right and half wrong. "And they only gave us a small amount of money," I added.

Molly then got up and looked at me and said, "You girls can stay here for the night. We can talk more about it in the morning." She said smiling.

"Thank you!" I said. I then turned around to tell Elizabeth about what sort of happened to us. She was seated down so I had to whisper it to her fast. She stared at me with an okay look. I then sat down next to her. Molly came into the room with the pot with a towel wrapped around it. It must still be hot. And behind her was the other little boy with the basket of biscuits.

She was going around the table one at a time scoping a spoon full of everyone's bowels. When she got to me, I saw that there were noodles and a darker meat. It didn't look like chicken. Molly was finished and sat down.

"Marty would you like to say a prayer," Molly asked her other daughter. Marty had long dark-brown hair. She was beautiful for her age as well.

"No mama I don't," she answered with her head down. Molly didn't fuss over that. Instead, she just went ahead and said it herself.

"Amen," we all said.

We then started to eat. The soup was hot and delicious, and the biscuits were warm. I haven't had a meal like this in a long time. I was so hungry that I ate every bite. I was finished before everyone else. Molly had the pot just sitting in the middle of the table. I tried to see if there were some more in there and there was. I barely got a good glimpse.

"May I have some more?" I asked my voice low. I was scared at first to ask I wasn't sure if I was allowed to have seconds for this is a really big family.

"Why yes child you may have some more to eat. We need to eat it up tonight. Eric will you help her?" Molly smiled.

"Yes mama," he cheered I think Eric is always in a good mood. The boys were on the other side of the table. I handed my bowel to Eric as he put a spoon full of soup in my bowel and another biscuit on top of it. He had to do it a few additional times as the other children wanted some more to eat.

"So girls where are you two from?" Molly asked. I was eating and so I was hoping Elizabeth would answer to that.

"We're from Indianapolis," Elizabeth said. The other girls gasped.

"Wow, the city!" Savanna said. I smiled at her. I just like to smile.

"Katherine and Elizabeth are going to stay the night with us children," Molly announced. "Why?" Marty asked? She's the one with dark-brown hair right I don't always have a good memory.

"Would you like to explain it to them?" Molly asked me.

"Sure," I started to say. "Elizabeth and our parents well kicked us out of our houses and we don't know why honestly," I explained to them, and it wasn't a truthfully good one either of the explaining. So I hope they get it to think it really happened.

"How sad, where are they going to be sleeping at, mama," one of the girls asked. She was at the other side of the table next to Ethan. She had long wavy light brown hair and she, and another boy is the only two I haven't gotten a name form.

"We'll see later, Madison." That's a beautiful name, *Madison*.

"So girls how did you like your supper?" Molly asked.

"It was really good, thank you," I said.

"Well we all pitched in to help make it. The boys set out trap's late last night and caught two rabbits this morning. And the girls helped me this afternoon to make the noodles," Molly said getting up. She and Eric were going around and were picking up all the dishes. Everyone here helps out a lot or they each have a part they do every day.

I saw Ethan get up from his chair and was walking over towards me. So then I got up.

"I'll go out and get your things," he said.

"Oh, I'll go with you," I said. We walked out of the house. He jumped onto the wagon and started sliding one trunk at a time. They weren't that heavy, and then he through our bags at me. I dropped mine, but I didn't say anything about it. When we got inside we placed our things by the staircase to move later. It was still daylight outside, and some of the kids went out to play.

"I'm going to put the wagon up; you can come if you want." He looked at me with a long gaze. I did like the looks of his brown eyes and freckles. He left, and I followed and outside we were again. We were walking toward the barn this time to get the horses. We only had to stop once for the kids to run pass us. As he was hooking up the horses, I was standing there watching him. He jumped up and reached out his arm saying, "Do you want a ride?" I looked at him thinking.

"Sure." And he helped me up. Okay I know it was a short ride but who cares.

After he put the wagon up and the horses, we walked back to the house slowly talking.

"Do you like my family?" he asked smiling.

"Yes, your family is kind and big." I laughed. We didn't go inside this time. Instead, we just sat down on the top step on the porch.

"Most of you don't look like each other," I said I think it was rude, but I'm not sure.

"Ha, yeah some of us aren't really related to Molly," he laughed. "Eric and I were adapted and so were Samuel and Jeffrey." Jeffrey, that's that other boy's name.

"Eric and I were five when both of our parents died from an illness. And Samuel and Jeffrey's parents…" he stopped talking and took a deep breath. "Well they died in a wagon accident. Both boys were at the neighbor's house. They were only two years old."

"And the girls," I asked.

"Molly was married to David Janes. That's Marty and Emma's father. After the girls were a year-old, he got really sick and died. However, Eric and I didn't know him because we weren't adapted yet." So there's not a father here. That's all I could think of.

"I was six at the time, and knew that Eric and I had to be the man around here. Molly then later got married to Justin Cooper the father of Madison and Savanna. The two of them were born on the same day but are not twins." He said.

"I'm confused?" I said looking at him, and then he turned his head towards me.

"Madison has a different mother whom she and everyone else have never seen or met besides Justin that one night."

"And so what happened to Justin?" I asked.

"Oh nothing happened to him; he's down in George visiting family." And now I feel stupid.

"And so that means out of all of you, Savanna is the only one that has both parents?" I asked.

"Ha, yeah," he laughed and then said softly. Its sunset now and I don't know what time it is?

"The only bad things I can remember about my parents were their names," he said sadly.

"What were they?" I asked softly.

"Well, my father's was Bryce Lee and my mother's was Hanna Lee," he said through a smile afterwards.

"We should go inside its getting dark," he then stood up quick.

"Jeffrey, Madison, Savanna, Samuel let's go inside now!" he yelled at them with his hands cupped around his mouth. He gave me a hand up, and we went inside. When we got into the dining room, Molly, Eric, and

Elizabeth was all sitting upon the sofa. Molly was reading a book and was talking to the both of them. Marty was sitting on the floor, and the children ran pasted Ethan and me to sit next to her. There was only one more spot to sit at on the sofa between Elizabeth and Eric but Ethan pulled out two chairs from the table for the both of us.

"Well I was thinking girls, Katherine and Elizabeth," she started. "That you two could sleep in a bed together in one of the girls beds. Maybe Savanna could sleep with Madison." It got quiet after that.

"Or mama, they can sleep with Ethan and me," Eric suggested. Yeah I guess he's the funny one around here. The girls all giggled.

"Well I'm not sure about that," Molly said.

"Oh mama let them; we all know they're all going to get married," Marty said and the girls smiled.

"Marty I don't want you to be saying anything else like that again you hear?" She said.

"Yes mama," she said sadly with her head down.

"We could go and sleep in one of the girl's beds," I suggested.

"All right that could work. Savanna, are you okay with giving up your bed. You could sleep with me tonight."

"Mama, can I sleep with you too." "I as well,'" the other three girls cheered.

"Well I guess so," she smiled. If my mama didn't have father she would let me sleep with her every night, and I know she would.

"Well I think it's getting late now. Off to bed children," Molly said as we all got up and were heading to where we all needed to go. "Good night boys!" she yelled.

"Good night mama," Eric and Ethan said at the same time as they were making their way to the staircase.

"Good night Katherine and Elizabeth."

"Good night Molly," we said. There were four doors in the small hallway. Eric was first in the line, imagine that. He turned left in the first door. It was dark at first then there was a glow in the room Eric was in. He came out to show us the room we were going to sleep in.

"I guess you two can get your own bed tonight since the girls are sleeping downstairs," Eric said.

"Or if you want you could still sleep with us," he laughed.

"Is there anything I could do for you before we hit the hay?" Eric asked.

"Yes, I would like my trunk up here," Elizabeth said. "Okay."

"Eric no, she's kidding you!" I laughed as he smiled.

"Oh, well I can still get it and yours as well." And he left. Elizabeth turned around quick and smiled.

"I think he could come in handy," she said. In the doorway, I saw Ethan there shirtless.

"Well good night girls if you need anything I'm in the other room across the hall, the same room with Eric. So good night, and good night Katherine," he said and then left. Eric was up here now with our things. He said his good nights to us.

"Good night Elizabeth," he said, and he then closed the door leaving the candle on the little table by the door. It had a tiny glow to it, and so we couldn't see much. I mean yes we could because it wasn't that dark outside. Elizabeth and I opened our trunks to get our nightgowns out. We've each has had the same dress on the last two days.

"See you in the morning Elizabeth," I said to her.

"He likes you, you know that."

"Who Ethan. No. Besides, Eric likes you a lot. The way he interrupted you when we all first met each other and when we got here he said, 'And this is the beautiful Elizabeth.' Right," I said as we both got in the beds and under the coverts.

"Ugh…" That was all she could say as she blew out the candle. And now I go to sleep.

Chapter 5

Don't you hate it when you're dreaming, and you think it was real, well that just happened to me? I was dreaming that father found me and was treating me and mama terribly. However, it's over now, and it wasn't real thank goodness. However, still father could find me; we're only the next town away from Indianapolis. Wait, what is the name of this town?

I rolled over to my side to see Elizabeth's bed. She was facing the wall still asleep. I moved to sit up. I was still tired but a little more awake. Last night when we came into the room, it was sort of dark. However, what there is in the room are a desk and a chair. And by the door was a dish on a small table next to the candle that Eric left. Well if I can smell breakfast now, then I guess I should get up and get dressed. I got out a white blouse and a brown skirt to wear today. I was quite getting dressed and walking out of the room. Once in the hallway, the boy's door was open. When I looked inside both weren't in there. Right as I get down the steps Ethan comes running up quietly.

"Oh hey, I was on my way to check on you." Just I, I thought?

"You and Elizabeth," he whispered after words. I believed he caught onto that.

"Oh well, she's still asleep."

"Ah, Molly has breakfast ready. Well in a few minutes, she will, and I was to get you two up."

"Well then I'll get her up and tell Molly that we'll be down in a moment," I whispered back.

"Ok then," he smiled and went down stairs.

As I was making my way to the bedroom, Elizabeth was sitting up in bed.

"Did we wake you?" I asked as she was yawning.

"Yes, yes you two did," she said getting out of bed. I walked over to the chair to sit down. I gazed above to see Elizabeth. She was getting out today's clothes. She grabbed her yellow blouse and her dark-blue skirt. Then I gave her, her privacy by looking out the window while she got dressed. When she was done she started brushing her hair.

"They have breakfast ready down stairs,"

"Oh they do," she was struggling with her bun. I left my hair in a braid so that it wouldn't get in my face. Once when she was ready, we made our way down stairs to meet the family. All the children were placing what little they had on the table, fried ham with biscuits and gravy. We then seated. All the children were in different places from last night. I guess they like to sit wherever they can get a seat. After we all took our seats, we then stared passing the food around the table.

"You girls sleep alright?" Molly asked.

"Yes very well," I answered.

"I was thinking sense we all didn't have much to do today we could think about how we are going to do the bedrooms," Molly said. There was a silence of us eating.

"I'm sorry. What are you saying?" I asked before taking a bite of my ham.

"My family and I were talking this morning, and we would like it if you two would stay longer here," Molly said after taking a drink from her cup. I slowly chewed my ham and looked over at Elizabeth.

"I guess what I am saying is that we want you two to move in with us!" she smiled. Elizabeth and I gave a blank glare to each other. We were both thinking of what to say.

"Molly please you don't have to do this," I answered.

"Girls I want to. There's not another town in a day's walk," she said staring us down. I didn't look at Elizabeth; I just nod and said, "Thank you, Molly," quietly and finished eating.

"So as I was saying our family now welcomes you two girls in!" she smiled and everyone else cheered around. I gave off a smile to let them know that I am happy to have a place to stay. It's just I fell that it isn't right for Elizabeth and I to lie to this family and then let them take us in under their wing.

"So now we need to go back and discuss about the rooms," Molly then added on.

"They could move in with us," Eric said softly. Molly looked up from her plate and narrowed her eyes at him. Eric quickly went back to eating.

"I wouldn't mind sleeping with Katherine and so the other two girls could still have a bed to their own," Elizabeth suggested.

"That could work, but who would be the one to give up their bed?" Molly asked.

"We were in the room second door to the right, and I was sleeping in the bed closest to the window. Whose bed was that?" I asked.

"Mine," Savanna I think said with a smile. "Madison and I could sleep in her bed, and those two can have mine," she said. I could tell that Molly was thinking about this.

"Yes, that could work but we'll still think about it a little more," she said.

The breakfast was really pleasant this morning. The maids are good at making biscuits, and mama is trying but Molly's were the best I've had.

"What are you children planning on doing today?" Molly asked.

"I was going to finish that patch I started yesterday for you, mama," Emma said.

"And Savanna, Marty, and I were going to play in the barn until you're ready for our help to make dinner," Madison said. It's like a morning retain for the family. They all need to say what and where they are going. I mean I see it so you would have a trustworthy family. I wouldn't want anything to happen to this family there too nice!

"Ethan and the boys and I were going out in the woods to see anything about our traps," Eric said.

"If you boys catch a rabbit let's hope it's a big fat juicy one," She said. Elizabeth and I didn't say much. We just eat our food and listened to their conversations. When everyone got finished, they all went their separate ways to do things. We all had to take our dishes and put them on the one little table in the kitchen.

Molly went out to fetch a bucket of water from the well to wash the dishes. She was washing them outside on the porch. She didn't ask but Elizabeth, and I went to help her.

"Would you like us to help? We could dry for you," I asked. She was sitting on the porch dunking them in the bucket and wiping them with a rag. She looked up at us and said, "Yes of course; you may help me." She handed us two dry towels and the wet dishes.

"I'd better start having you two working hard since you'll be living here." I only smiled to that. Elizabeth laughed at this moment a bit.

The four boys walked out the door and started heading into the woods. They had a long walk out there. Eric and Ethan looked back at Elizabeth and me and smiled. I was watching how he walks; so manly but yet so gentle. The noises around me were fading as he kept on walking further and further away from me.

Katherine?

Katherine?

Was that my name being called out again?

"Katherine," Molly yelled even though she was right next to me.

"Yes sorry," I apologized.

"Were you daydreaming?" she asked. I stared at her with a blank face.

"She intends on doing that sometimes," Elizabeth answered for me.

"She's right." As I looked forward to finding the boys, they were long gone in the woods.

"You weren't watching by boys or one of my boys now was you?"

"No, well, um…" I didn't know what to say. She handed me a dish to dry. I was thinking about changing the subject, but yet we really weren't on one yet.

"We could say I was watching one of them," I teased. They just laughed.

"Yes it was Samuel that I was watching walking away." We all laughed. It then got quite a moment of sadness or something. I only had one question that I wanted to ask Molly.

"How do you do it? Having to handle all the children?" she looked up at me and handed Elizabeth another dish the last one.

"Well just like my mother she always got up with a smile and went on with the day no matter what she thought was coming." Good answer.

"What really helped me was that I had Ethan and Eric with me. Ethan told me this morning about what you two were talking about last night," she said.

"So were they your smile in the morning?" I asked. She looked at me with her green eyes and smiled.

"Yes."

"I have just one quick question to ask you," I paused. "What's the name of the town you live in?"

"Greenfield," she answered.

"Indianapolis is the next town then heading west," Elizabeth said, I was hoping she wasn't going to give away our lie; we have. However, Molly didn't question us which I'm glad. We were finished with what we were working on. She allowed us to do a few things that we wanted to do on our own. I went up stairs to write in my diary. There was a desk in the room, so I just sat there and wrote.

June 2, 1860 Morning

Dear Diary,

You won't believe the past few days I've had. Starting with June 1, Elizabeth and I, came upon a town called Greenfield. It's the next town away from Indianapolis. Mama told us that we needed to head east which we were at the time until I had my accident. A mad man on a wagon was coming towards me and would have run me over until someone saved me. Ethan Lee was the young man who saved me. He has short brown hair and brown eyes with freckles. Nevertheless, I see no future with him. He has a twin brother, Eric and I think he's fond Elizabeth. And that I see a future of the two of them.

We had to lie to their family saying that both of our families kicked us out. This family is very big. Molly is the mother of eight with a husband. Samuel and Jeffrey are the two youngest and the youngest boys. They were both two when their parents died. Savanna and Madison were born on the same day but are not twins. Each has the same father. It's Madison who has the different mother whom she, and everybody has not seen except her father. Emma and Marty are the next older girls who are both twins. They have a different father who has passed a long time ago. And then there's Ethan and Eric. They were five when Molly took them under her wing.

I feel like I'm talking too much about this family. I guess it's okay because I have nothing better to say. The four boys all left to go to the woods to check on the traps they left out yesterday. And the girls were going to play in the barn. I'm just up in the room that Elizabeth, and I are going to share together soon. We still haven't decided on where we're all are going. I honestly have nothing else to say anymore so I am going to do whatever that will be needed done.

Love Katherine

...

"Now what," I thought out loud. Either way if I said it in my head, it would have sounded strange. I think I'm eerie and so do Elizabeth. I put my diary away in my bag. My trunk was on the bed, and I want to move it but don't know where to? There's room under the bed but like I said before we all don't know where we are all going to be at. So I'm going to move it under the bed. While I'm moving it under, I spotted a small wooden box under the bed. I don't think it belongs to Savanna. It sure was under there in the very back. I had to get down on my stomach to reach that bad boy out.

There was a lot of dust around it. There was a name engraved on it saying, Molly Tyler. I bet that was her first husband's last name.

"Katherine? You up there," It was Ethan at the bottom of the stairs. He was coming up.

"In here," I yelled. I moved the box back where it was originally and quickly sat on the bed like I wasn't getting into anything. The door moved slowly as he popped his head in.

"Hey," he smiled. I still don't feel anything for him. Random for me to say I thought.

"Hello," I smiled back.

"We just got back." He paused to sit on the other bed. He cleared his throat like he was nerves to even talk to me.

"We caught a squirrel and a rabbit. Sam was happy about the squirrel because it was on the trap that I helped him with," he laughed and okay yes; it was cute when he said Sam. It was short for Samuel. I just smiled and nodded along.

"Uh huh," just keep smiling. I don't mind having Ethan for company. I think the reason he's up here with me is to get to know me better. Oh I wish I could keep up with the time. I wonder if he likes my company? Maybe I should ask a few questions just so it doesn't get awkward for us soon.

"What's Molly's husband's last name?"

"What Justin's, Cooper," he answered.

"And what was her first husband's last name?"

"Janes," he answered. Wait, on the box it said Tyler and now her last name is wait, I can't remember?

"Okay wait isn't her last name Luke was it, and so wouldn't it be Cooper?" I asked because I'm confused.

"Well after her first husband's death, she went back to her maiden name. And then she had all of us kids just stay with our last names. The boys are Underwood; the girls are Janes, and the other girls are Cooper."

So where does Tyler come in at? Perhaps I'm getting this all wrong. Possibly it could have been her grandpa's name or her great grandpa's name. I have my great grandma's name.

"Why did you want to know about everyone's last names?" I think he could be getting on to me. Maybe he doesn't know anything about the box.

"Oh just wanted to get to know your family a little better that's all," I answered.

"Should we go down stairs?" he asked while getting up.

"Yes," I answered him. He was the first one out and down the stairs. We walk into the family room as he makes his way to sit down at the table. I walk into the kitchen to see what's going on.

Molly was already getting started for dinner.

"Ah Katherine I need your help," Molly asked while mixing in a bowl. It's only been an hour since we ate last. Back at home after breakfast I would be in my room watching the city or in the study reading. I guess I never truly knew how much our maids did work hard day after day.

"I'm a little rusty," true about that.
"No bother we can help," she smiled.
"And Elizabeth is the same Molly," I added.
"Like I said no bother." She smiled.

Chapter 6

June 5, 1860 Afternoon

Dear Diary,

Elizabeth and I have been living at the Luke, Cooper, Janes, Underwood, and Lee's house in the last three days. I don't know how to put what to call this place. In the last three days, Elizabeth and I learned how to milk the cow. It's really weird because we should already know how to, but we live or lived in the city. Plus our maids did all the work with the animals.

My relationship with Ethan is still the same. I, however, feel as if he gets nerves every time he talks to me. Eric is still trying to get Elizabeth's attention. He has my attention. Lately he's been saying a few jokes here and there, and I laugh to all of them. I think he's humorous and then theirs Ethan, who is slowly saying a few around me. This family is very amusing.

Ever sense I've been here Molly has been the first one up and would be fixing breakfast. However, this morning she was the last one up. So we children made breakfast. Later, Ethan was out in the barn moving things. I asked him if he knew if Molly was okay. He had said that around this time every year she was always down. There has to be something going on with her? Well my diary I have to go. Really no reason but I can't think of anything else to write about.

Love Katherine

...

Like every day I close my book and put it away in my bag. I'm feeling a bit tired so I think I'll go lie down.

...

Katherine?

Am I dreaming still or was it Ethan? I opened one eyes to see who it was.

"Samuel," My voice was soft. He was kneeling in front of me. He was smiling too. What is on this little boy's mind that could be so important that he had to wake me up?

"Are you okay? Do you need me? Does Ethan, Molly, or Elizabeth need me?" I asked him. He was a little blur that I was trying to make out because I'm still trying to wake up. He just looks at me at the same time smiling.

"No, I came up here to play with my toys and saw you sleeping. I wanted to wake you up," great answer I thought. I think Eric is rubbing on to him.

"You want to play with me?" he asked. I sat up as he got up on his feet. He was about to jump on the bed as I reached my arms out to sit him next to me.

"Maybe later, I promise little man," he just looks up at me with those light-blue eyes of his and smiles.

"Supper is almost ready. You want to go down stairs?" he asked.

"Why of course," I laughed.

Samuel was holding my hand all the way down. I didn't mind it, and I liked it a lot. From looking out of one of the windows supper was a little late. It was almost sun set. No one asked me *yet* what happened to me in the last few hours. The older boys just smiled at me and went on setting up the table. Marty and Madison were already seated. Samuel sat next to me, figures. Molly and the other girls came in the room with our food.

Rabbit stew and rolls what looks to be. We all started to pass the bowls around and bowed our heads.

"Dear Lord, bless this food and this house for that we will be safe. Amen." I think Eric could have done better with the prayer. We then started to eat. Every meal either Molly or one of the older boys will say a prayer. And also they go to church. We've already had gone once with them. We went to the St. Michael's Catholic Church. My family never went to church. Now I really wish we would have.

"I have some news children," Molly said. We all looked up at her. And when I mean we all that includes Elizabeth and I.

"What is it mama?" Emma asked.

"Pal's coming home tomorrow," she smiled. The children all cheered.

"Really," Jeffrey cheered.

"Yes really. I got a letter a few days ago saying he'll be home June 6. And tomorrow's going to be the 6th." Molly said. We all finished eating. She got up and grabbed all the plates. The boys ran to their room and seconds later they came back with a few of their toys in their arms. The girls already had a few of their dolls by the chairs and were playing with them.

Ethan was lighting some candles in the room. After supper, we all sit and talk in the family room together. It's just a few last minutes of family time before bedtime. This was a first to see Elizabeth and Eric sitting next to each other. I was going to sit next to Ethan when I saw Samuel giving me a gaze. I did promise to play with him. I got down on my butt to play with him and Jeffrey.

They had six soldiers and four soldiers on horses. I bet their pal made them or Eric and Ethan. Ethan came and sat down and was watching me or the boys. It was just us kids in the family room; Molly was cleaning the dishes alone.

"What are you looking at?" I asked Ethan. He just smiles.

"I'm looking at you," he said so calm. I've been here five days, and now he saw my beauty? On the other hand, he might only be looking at me because I was playing with the boys. He then got down on his knees and was playing as well.

"Now these guys are your cowboys. You don't want to mess with them when you go out west," he explained to them.

"Who's going out west?" I asked.

"They both are when they have the money and equipment they need when they get older," he said as the boy's nodded their heads.

"And women!"

"Whoa Jeffrey not yet," Ethan laughed and the rests of us were doing the same.

I glanced over to see Elizabeth and Eric. They were talking, and she was actually smiling for the first time just being around him. I think things are changing for her.

"Katherine you're going to be a cowboy and so is Ethan," Jeffrey said to me. I was smiling and said, "Why do I have to be a cowboy? Ethan said they were the bad guys."

"Because that's how it's going to be," he said and went on playing. I've never played with boys ever, only Elizabeth and an old friend who moved. I thought it was charming when Ethan was playing with his younger brothers. There's still are no feelings for him.

"What happened to you after dinner?" Ethan had to ask.

"I found her sleeping," thanks Samuel.

"Sleeping," Ethan questioned.

"Yes I was a bit tired so I went to lie down," I said.

"It's okay I do that sometimes, like after a hard day working out in the fields," he said. I think he's doing it again. He's nervous to talk to me, and he's saying random things.

"Bed time children," Molly said coming in the room. It's still too early to go to bed. Well, I did just wake up a while ago from sleeping a little.

"Why mama," Savanna asked.

"We need our sleep." She said quickly. All of us children got up and started heading up stairs. All four girls went into their one room since Elizabeth, and I took Savanna's and Madison's room. The older boys were helping the younger boys into their beds.

"Good night Katherine. Thanks for keeping your promise," Samuel said waving good night to me while he was heading for his room.

"Any time," I said to him. I was still standing in the middle of the doorway of my room. Why am I doing that? Am not waiting for Ethan to say good night? Eric came out and put a hand on my shoulder smiling and saying, "Tell Elizabeth I said good night to her. She ran off before I could say it." I gave a little laugh while nodding my head saying, "I will."

And then he left me. Just before entering his room, he took off his shirt and through it in his room. He looked good without it. He was all muscle. I don't understand why Elizabeth hasn't felt anything for him. I see it as the same with me and Ethan, I feel nothing for him. There was the candle light in the hallway so that made me see him better. He was just standing there in his doorway, why? He gave me a glance over his shoulder.

"Eric," Called out the girls. I forgot the girls like a good-night kiss from one of their big brothers.

Ethan finally came out. He stopped in front of me really close, almost too close. I could smell his breath. I liked the smell of it because that is how he smells. It wasn't a nasty smell, but it also wasn't a clean smell either. My heart was pounding really fast for the first time I've been here, why?

"What did you promise Samuel?" he asked.

"He wanted me to play with him, and I said I would wait until another time," I said. He was quiet, just standing there staring at me with those brown eyes of his.

"I feel like hugging you," he whispered and why does he want to hug me? One of his hands was holding mine. His hand was warm.

"Instead of hugging. How about you do something different," I subjected. Why did I just say that? He was leaning in closer. I could feel his breath on my lips, until Eric came out of the girl's room. Ethan pulled back quickly, and we both were looking at him. Luckily, I had the door closed for Elizabeth to change. Eric gave out a pitiful laugh and walked on into his room. Ethan looked at me with a blank face and walked away closing the door behind him. He just left me out in the hallway, why?

I blew out the two candles from the hallway; the candle hanging on the wall and the candle sitting on the desk at the end of the hallway. I opened the door to find Elizabeth writing in her diary. I got out my nightgown to sleep in and then moved the sheets to get in bed. I laid my head down on my pillow and was watching her write.

"What are you looking at?" she asked. I gave her smile.

"You, and you can write this down, Eric said to me in his words, 'Tell Elizabeth good night, and that I love her.'"

"He did not say that, gosh!" she yelled well not yelled she just raised her voice and through one of her pillows at me. She did give me a big smile one that even showed some teeth. She then was done writing and blew out a candle. I did the same over on the desk. I was all covered up and had to lean all the way over to blow out the candle. I turned to facing the wall and tried to go to sleep but couldn't. My heart was still pounding hard. I've never felt like this way ever before.

. . .

I still haven't gone to sleep, and I know hours have had to go by. I wonder if Ethan is sleeping or a wake. I'm yawning so that must mean I'm about to fall asleep.

. . .

I know for a fact that was one of my longest nights yet. I didn't get much sleep. Its early morning and when I say early I mean I got up early. Elizabeth got up at the same time as well. We got out of bed, got dressed, and then went down stairs. Molly was up with a cup of coffee in her hands. The boys were either still in their room or out in the barn milking and collecting eggs. Today was when Molly's husband comes home.

"The boys already left to town," she said.

"Oh," I was surprised. She got up and was walking towards the small table in the kitchen and handed Elizabeth a bucket and me a basket.

"We need milk and eggs," she said. I think we hesitated to walk out of the house.

"Now I wish the boys were here," Elizabeth said.

"You don't mean just Eric?" I said. She gave me a smile.

"Uh no," then she started walking faster than me.

From being here the last few days and watching Ethan in the barn, I now know the name of the animals. Bessie the cow and the three horses are Chester, Buck, and Roller.

"Do you think you'll be okay with Bessie?" I asked her.

"Yes, I think I'll be. I'll holler for you if I need help." And she went over to Bessie. Buck and Roller were gone with the boys. I had to go get the eggs. The chicken coop wasn't in the barn but next to it outside.

I came back to see Elizabeth half sock in wet and with only a half a bucket of milk.

"I hollered for you!" she raised her voice. I laughed, and she was doing the same as well.

"You think it's funny? What happened to you?" I asked.

"No I'm laughing at you."

"What," I was covered with chicken feathers. Now we were putting what happened to us behind and was just laughing at each other. We were walking to the house with what little Elizabeth has, and I had.

"What happened, Elizabeth? Your hands were maybe too cold," Molly raised her voice.

"Go, go wash up!" She yelled while taking the bucket of milk and basket of eggs away from us. Maybe she was mad at us for looking like this, or she was panicking about her husband coming home. Elizabeth was washing the milk off her face and arms. I took off all the feathers that were on me. I got out some new clean clothes to wear. I got out her a blouse with her bark brown skirt. I sort of had to change as well. I had chicken crap on the hem of my skirt. So I had to get my white blouse and light blue skirt.

"Here let me do your hair," I said moving her to the chair. I brushed her hair back in a braid. She did the same to mine. When we came in the house a little earlier the girls were playing in the family room with their dolls. Elizabeth and I sat at the table to talk and watch. We later went to help Molly out.

…

Hours have gone by maybe two hours I would say. The men just got back. Eric came in first then Ethan. The children all ran out to hug their pal. He looked to be a few years' elderly than Molly. I would say about seven years if so. He had a short full beard and some nice clothes on. I would say this family is not that rich but poor so maybe he had to of gotten his clothes from someone he knows? They all came in shortly after words. He came in and kissed Molly. He looked at Elizabeth, and I confused.

"Pal this is Elizabeth," Eric said standing next to her. Ethan was doing the same standing next to me.

"And this is…" he stopped. Why did Ethan stop? I'm just going on to say my own name, "Katherine."

There's quite starting again.

"I'm making your favorite a whole ham!" Molly said. Eric, Elizabeth, Ethan, and I went into the other room to give the family some space to catch up. We all sat on the sofa together.

"Ha, Ethan couldn't remember Katherine's name," Eric said quietly but loud enough for Ethan to hear. It went Eric then Elizabeth, different than me and Ethan all sitting down. I reached over Elizabeth to punch him in the arm. He gave out a pity noise. Elizabeth went to whisper something in his ear, "Stop."

Molly came in the room, "Supper's going to be a little late."

"But mama we haven't had at least dinner yet," Eric complained.

"I thought you would say that Eric. When you boys were out picking up your father, I per sliest some ham and fried it. You four can go up stairs to eat." Wow she's going to let us eat up stairs? She came back with a plate of fired ham slices and some biscuits. Eric of cores took the plate, and the rest of us followed him to his room.

"Either of you, two ate breakfasts," Ethan asked.

"Yeah," Elizabeth said. We wolfed down our meal. Elizabeth and Eric were sitting on his bed. Eric must have told her a joke because the two were laughing.

"I want to talk to you, alone," Ethan whispered to me as he grabbed my hand ever so gently. I had no time to say okay we just went.

He closed the door behind him, but I don't think that's going to work for the two not to hear us?

"I'm sorry about what almost happened last night."

"Don't be, we didn't even *kiss*," I whispered.

"Well I'm still sorry." Okay have it your way then.

"I couldn't sleep," he whispered.

"Same here," I whispered back. We went to the room to all talk some more.

Molly hollered up the stairs for us to tell us that supper is ready. It must have been a while.

0 "Yeah supper I'm hungry!" Eric yelled.

"Eric you're always hungry," Elizabeth laughed. We all sat down to say our prayers. Justin started us off for the night. Molly baked ham and a loaf of bread with butter for the bread. We weren't allowed to talk because Justin was the only one allowed to talk. I can see why because he was talking about his trip down in Georgia visiting his friend. Around the end of dessert which we also haven't had since Elizabeth, and I have been here at the house; the boys finally had a chance to tell Justin about Elizabeth and I of why we are here, and that we are staying.

Justin was staring at Elizabeth and me, why?

"So girls I don't mind you two living here as long as you help out with the working," he said. The rest of the family all laughed.

"Oh we've been doing our fair share of the work don't you worry sir," I said.

"Pleas just call me Justin." Okay then I thought. Some of the girls were asking him a few questions about George. And then the questions went to Elizabeth and me.

"So, um I can't seem to remember your name's girls?" he asked.

"Elizabeth and I am, Katherine."

"Oh, so you aren't sisters are you?" he asked.

"No just friends," Elizabeth answered.

"Do you have any siblings?"

"I have an older brother, Logan, but we haven't talked in years and Katherine…"

"I'm an only child," I said quickly and interrupted Elizabeth. She was staring at me. Then the questions went back to Justin about George. Justin only had what little time to ask questions to Elizabeth and me because of his children. I really didn't mind the questions. It gives him a chance to get to know us a little more.

It was time for all of us to go to bed for the night. We were all way too tried to talk some more. The boys went to put the children to bed while Elizabeth, and I helped Molly wash the dishes. When we were finished, we walked up to bed. Eric was waiting by our door to tell Elizabeth good night. She stopped and actually said good night to him and then went on.

I got nothing from Ethan. How am I supposed to feel about it? I guess nothing until if I do feel something for him. I'm too tired to think now. I had a hard time to get dressed because I'm so tired. My bed was soft like if I was sleeping on a cloud. Sometimes when I'm so tired I just mumble off random things until I have fallen to sleep.

Chapter 7

July 1, 1860 afternoon

Dear Diary,

June 7th, June 8th and so on until July 1st. Ethan still hasn't kissed me yet. I am in misery. What am I to do? Do I have feelings for him? We almost kissed that one night but didn't. So I can't have feelings for him. Molly and the children and Justin all went to town to get a few supplies. Ethan and Eric staid back with Elizabeth and me. They had to work on a few things in the barn. In the last few days, Emma has been teaching Elizabeth to sew. My cooking has been getting better as well.

However, about Ethan, we still talk. Sometimes we've sat next to each other when eating. Nevertheless, the boys always want to sit next to me. I was just looking out my window and saw a deer. She was big and beautiful. She's still standing there eating. I'm going to stop writing to watch her eat.

...

I then closed my book and put it away for the day maybe. Still sitting at the desk, I ran my hand across the surface of it. I wanted to feel the roughness of the hard wood. Then I glanced down and pulled my hand away from it.

"Ouch!" I yelled. I had a splinter in my finger. I need Ethan to check this out. I got up from my chair and ran down stairs to find Ethan. Once outside I saw him walking up to the house from the barn.

"Ethan," I yelled at him as he was coming up dragging some rope behind him.

"What?"

"I need you to look at my hand," I started to say holding my hand up until he interrupted me by saying, "Is everything okay?"

"No. I have a splinter stuck in it." He then dropped the rope and yanked my hand to see it himself.

"Hmm," he'd say then adding on, "Let's sit here on the porch." He walked me to the porch, and we sat down.

He held my hand up close to his eye to see it a little closer.

"Okay here is what I'm going to do," he started to say then paused.

"Does it hurt?" he asked. I stare him down and think to myself. Yeah it hurts if not, I wouldn't come to you for help. All I just say is, "Yes it hurts." Next he finished saying, "I'm going to do this, okay…" and after that he sticks my finger into his mouth and tried to take the splinter out by that way. I could feel his teeth and his tongue. He narrowed his eyes while he was doing this. I didn't know what to look at but him.

After that he pulled my finger out of his mouth and wiped off his spit with his shirt. He next held my hand not even looking at it but at me. We gazed into each other's eyes. Ethan then looked down at my hand to see my finger while saying, "There I think I got it."

"Thank you, Ethan," I say to him, but he didn't let go of my hand. He kept a grip of it.

"When Molly gets back we'll have her look at your finger. We won't want it to get infected," he said then letting go of my hand.

"I need to get back to work," he said standing up then turning around to help me up.

"I've somehow lost Eric!" he laughed. I smile and say, "Yeah I lost Elizabeth too." We both laughed at who we lost just now.

"Well I need to go," he says then walks away. I decide to head back inside just to sit in the family room. I make my way to sit at the table. I sit here a lot just thinking and listening to what the family has to say about things. I realize that I want my mama. I miss her. I'm thinking about writing a letter to mama, but later to night.

Where's Elizabeth? I haven't seen her all day? Maybe she's out in the barn talking to Eric? I get up from my seat and start walking out of the house. As I was walking to the barn, I didn't see Ethan anywhere working. So maybe he might be in the back field checking on traps or something. Once in the barn, I didn't see her anywhere. I looked in the bottom, and then I climbed up to the loft. She was nowhere to be found. As I got back down from being on the ladder, I went on around the back of the barn. I slowed down just before making the turn. I pocked my head to see, and it was a shocking surprise. Elizabeth and Eric were kissing. I jolt back quick. I didn't think that I made a sound, but maybe I did. I heard Elizabeth say, "Did you hear something?" Eric said, "No."

I slowly walked back to the house. I was surprised that I saw that. While walking to the house I had to remember to breathe. I'm feeling happy and light headed also. Once in the house again, I go back and sit at the table and wait until someone comes in to talk. I've been sitting at the table for maybe fifteen minutes until I hear the family coming up from the drive. Molly walks in then the girls follow behind her. I'm just sitting at the table until someone comes in and talks to me. I realize I don't ever have anything to do here besides to help cook and or write in my diary. Other than that I never have anything to do.

"Ah Katherine how are you?" Molly asked as she came walking in the family room. What do I say, 'oh I'm great,' 'I'm fine,' I don't know?

"I'm okay," I swallowed hard after answering her.

"Are you hungry?"

"Yes."

"Looks like we'll have deer to night then," she said. I wonder how we'll have deer unless Ethan came back with a deer. Maybe that's where he ran off to, I don't really know?

"Sounds great," I say. Savanna came running in towards me. She stands next to me staring me down with a smile from ear to ear on her face.

"Katherine, Katherine, Katherine!" Savanna kept on saying my name so excited.

"Savanna, slow down," I tried to calm her. "What is it?" I asked.

"When we were in town you won't believe who I saw there, Nate Wells!" She kept on going.

"Wait who is he?" I asked wondering.

"Oh just a boy I really like."

"How old is he?" I asked. She just smiled at me. "C'mon Savanna you can tell me how old he is."

"He just turned fifteen," she said quickly.

"Savanna your only how old are you again," I said.

"I'm thirteen," she answers.

"Oh," I only say.

The other girls came in but then started walking up stairs.

"Don't say anything to them, please," she looked at me with those big eyes of hers.

"I won't. I have a question though? Has Ethan ever been in love before?"

"Not to my knowledge?" she answered then said, "Why you asking?"

"Oh I just wanted to know if so or not," I say.

"Okay then."

"Thanks," and then she left to go up stairs.

I was a bit nerves to ask, but I was brave, or so I thought? Molly came walking in stopping at the dinning-table then putting both hands face flat down on it. It looks to be that she was getting all her thoughts in one place in order to say something.

"Molly," I say to her getting her attention.

"Ah, I just remembered that I forgot to get something at the general store. Would you like to come with me after breakfast?" she asked. I don't know about this it's been a month since I've been out to town.

"Yeah I would love to come," I answered her. She gave me a smile then said, "Good the boys will take us later." Then she left for the kitchen. Wait the boys, meaning Ethan? Well, I guess I could go write mama's letter. However, the only paper I have is from my diary, and I really don't want to tear any out. However, I want mama to know Elizabeth, and I am okay, so I think I'll go write that letter now.

When walking up stairs, I could hear the girls playing with their dolls. It sounded cute. Marty and Emma are of the age of fourteen I believe and are still playing with dolls. When I was fourteen I snuck-around with

Elizabeth and a few friends. Good memories of child age. When I got in my room, I stared hunting my diary.

"Where is it?" I panicked. I just had it this morning before I hurt myself. Oh and I never did have Molly look at my finger. Oh well maybe in a little while I'll have her look at it. I looked in my bag, on the bed and under the bed but nothing. Then I looked on the desk, and it was there. I remembered that I left it there from earlier. I sat down and went to the last page and tore it out. I then started to write.

July 1, 1860

Dear Mama,

It's Katherine. Elizabeth and I are fine and safe. I know you wanted us to head east which we did but only the next town away. We are staying with a really nice family in Greenfield. There are two twin brothers who are a month older than Elizabeth and two months older than me. Eric Lee is the younger one and at the beginning when we first met him, he felt something for Elizabeth. She at first didn't feel anything but yet today I saw them kissing behind the barn.

About a month ago Ethan and I did feel something. One night he was about to kiss me until Eric came into the hallway. And until then I have more feelings for him. Mama I didn't tell you this at the beginning but the day we met the brothers was when Ethan saved my life. I was out in the middle of the road when a mad man in a speeding wagon was racing towards me. I fell and could not get up. Ethan came running after me and saved me. Mama I have feelings for him because he saved me.

And mama, Elizabeth and I lied to the family saying that you, and father kicked us out of the house and so did the Kent's as well. We are fine and safe. Oh mama I miss you. I've been getting better on my cooking; Molly is the mother, and she's been helping Elizabeth and me. Mama I love you and hope to see you soon if not.

Love Katherine

. . .

Writing this letter was hard for me. I didn't put much emotion in it, but she'll understand I hope. Do I tell Molly that I have a letter to mail to my mama? I mean what if mama writes back? Maybe I should add to the letter to tell her not to write back for certain reasons.

...

And mama, please don't write back to me for certain reasons I love you.

...

There I am done writing. And I won't tell Molly about this. Now I only need to put this in my bag, so I have it tomorrow. At the moment, I am only looking out the window until Molly calls for me to let me know that supper is done. An hour later, Molly calls for me.

I didn't say this before but a few days ago Molly gave Elizabeth and I a bible to read. I've been reading it to know what to say. On the first page, it says Manual of Catholic Devotions. This is a Catholic family. Molly then calls for me and the girls also. I walk out and lead the way down stairs. While walking I could see Ethan and Eric setting up the table. I would watch them both. Elizabeth came in with the rolls as Molly came in with our main dishes. We all took our seats and bowed our heads as Justin said the prayer. We then started passing around the dishes. I had forgotten that we were going to have deer. Molly made it into a stew. It tasted great.

I glanced over to see Ethan. He wasn't eating much. I was eating and afterwards listening to everyone's conversations. The girls would be talking, and the younger boys would be talking to each other. Eric and Elizabeth would be talking to Molly. I am still suppressed about what I saw. I really feel the need to tell this to Ethan. Oh yeah Ethan! He was sitting on the other side of the table next to Justin. Justin was talking to him, but Ethan didn't say much. He was just sitting there eating. He was also staring at me. Why? Well, I was doing the same. We were talking with our eyes it seemed like.

After supper Molly, Elizabeth, and I cleaned up the table. The girls help also. All the men and the younger ones all sat in the family room and started talking. After we all got finished, we joined them. I sat down at the table like always. We never seem to have enough places to sit.

"I need some air," I said standing up then left. As I'm leaving I could hear Molly say, "Okay."

And then there's Ethan, "I think I'll go too." Why is he coming? I didn't even wait for him to leave the door open for him. It was still daylight. I was sitting on the top step waiting for him.

"What is with you today?" he yelled slamming the door close. His lovely brown eyes narrowed.

"I don't know what you're talking about?" I lied I do know what he is talking about. He put his hands on his head and then started passing.

"Oh I know you know Katherine Stone! You've been acting all weird this past month. Let me guess was it because I haven't been sitting next to you when it's time to eat?" he kept on going.

"No," I answered him then got up and started walking towards the barn. He was following me still babbling on. He was following me as we walked.

"Is it because I've stopped saying good night you at night?"

"No," I answered as I walked in the barn. I next started climbing the latter up to the hay loft. He was holding my waist as I was climbing, and afterwards he started to come up. I was standing there waiting for him again. Why does he even bother? He next got close to me like that one night. He then started to smile.

"Was it because of that kiss that didn't happen?" he smiled and then came in so fast that I didn't even see it coming. He kissed me.

Time is frozen for me. He then pulled back. I was shocked. And why is he smiling?

"You do know why I'm mad at you!" I yelled at him as he was laughing. How could he go from acting all mad about then laughing?

"Yes, and you should have seen your face!" he laughed harder. I then started to laugh.

"Ethan Lee you play a hard game," and he then leaned closer holding my hands. We were kissing again, not stopping. I pulled away to say, "Why that one night you said you wanted to hug me?"

"I don't know why I said that? The wrong words came out," he hesitated. We then were sitting on the wooden floor just talking.

"Earlier, I saw Eric and Elizabeth kissing," I said finally getting that off my chest.

"No really," he said putting a hand on my knee. It was warm.

"He can't stop talking about her, you know."

"Well she hasn't said anything about him."

"We need to do something, anything to let them know that we know about them," he subjected.

"Your right," I answered him. We were lying back on the hay staring up at the ceiling. He had me all wrapped in his arms.

We've been up here in the hay loft for about an hour or so. The only thing we heard around us was the animals. We left the doors open, but we heard some kind of different noise from down below.

"Did you hear that?" he whispered getting up slowly.

"Eric and Elizabeth!" we whispered at the same time. We got up as slowly as we could without making any noise. Still hiding we could see the two kissing in the middle of the barn. We moved back quickly before they could even see us.

"Now we have proof!" he whispered. Yes, we have proof but now we're stuck up here. Maybe I should say that to him?

"Hey, we have proof, but now we're stuck up here." His smile went away after I said that.

"Damn it!" he whispered.

We waited for maybe five minutes to look down.

"They're gone," I whispered. We were whispering still because we weren't for sure if they were gone or not.

"Well it's getting dark. I'd rather take the risk than to have Molly yell at us." He went down the latter first to then help me down. He was such a gentleman and strong. Should I even say that? After helping me down we brushed all the hay that we found on us off and then ran to the house laughing. When we were on the porch, he stopped in front of the door. We both leaned in for one last kiss for the night. After going through the door we were walking quietly through. Molly was still up cleaning the dishes. I looked over at the clock that said eight.

"Eric and Elizabeth were looking for you two," she said to us. I looked over to Ethan. We gave the same gaze to each other saying that they weren't looking for us.

"Oh well, we took a long walk out back," Ethan lied. Molly looked over towards me, and I gave her a nod meaning yes.

"Okay then. Since you, four were all outside the children all put themselves to bed," she said. We then left her in the kitchen.

"Hey she did yell at us," I whispered.

"Actually, she didn't yell, she... Well okay have it your way, your right," he whispered. We went up stairs at different times so that Eric and Elizabeth wouldn't notice anything. Before, we both walked in our rooms we gave each other one last smile and wave good night.

When I walked into our room, Elizabeth was writing in her diary. She likes to write more at night but sometimes in the afternoon like I do.

"Eric and I were looking for you two?" she lied I know those two weren't looking for us.

"Yeah um we went for a walk out back," I lied. There's been a lot of laying going on around here tonight.

"Oh?" she said and went back to writing. I got dressed and brushed my hair. I found a piece of hay stuck in my hair. I hid it quick, so she wouldn't find it. Scheming, isn't it fun? We then blew out the candles and went to sleep.

...

This morning was feeling different. I woke up with a smile on my face maybe because I know Ethan will be pleased to see me. I know I'll be pleased to see him! I got out my light pink blouse with my brown skirt to wear today. I then just braided my hair back. I had a few lose pieces, which were alright. Elizabeth just got up and was washing her face. As I was leaving the room, I smiled at her and closed the door. The boy's door was open just a bit. I opened it up to see if they were in there. Eric without a shirt was laying on his stomach sound asleep. But know Ethan.

I was about to take a step on down the stairs until a hand came covering my mouth. I made a little noise then turned to see who it was. It was Ethan of course. He smiled at me while giving out a little laugh.

"You could have made me fall!" I whispered. He was still laughing but quiet though.

"No matter what I'll be there to save you," he whispered. He was leaning in until we heard one of the door's open. He pushed back and turned to see who it was. Eric came out still without a shirt on. He looked tired.

"Hey!" he said waving and still half asleep.

"Eric you look tired. How about you go back to bed, and I'll do your chores until breakfast," Ethan said to his brother.

"Okay thanks brother," and he left to go back to sleep in his bed. Ethan and I went on down stairs. Molly was up already making coffee.

"Eric was looking really tired so I made him go back to bed mama," he said to her. Molly gave a half smile to us.

"I was going to finish his chores only until breakfast."

"Well okay then. I hope he's not catching anything?" she said.

"Katherine's going to help me mama," he said quickly.

"Oh, okay maybe I'll have Elizabeth and the girls help me fix breakfast then."

We went out the door to go outside. While walking to the barn we were laughing hard. Ethan handed me the basket to go collect eggs while he milks Bessie. The chickens and I still haven't gotten along with each other. I'm just not used to collecting eggs every day that's why. I was done before he was. Milking takes a while I guess?

"Do you think Eric was really tried or was he acting like it, so he and Elizabeth could kiss or something?" I asked. Ethan turned his freckled head over towards me. I say that because he has lots of freckles on his face.

"You know I was thinking the same thing. So that is why I let him go back to sleep," he said and then went back to milk. Justin was coming out already.

"Justin's coming!" I whispered panicking.

"Why are you whispering?" he asked while whispering.

"Because I don't think he likes me?"

"Oh he likes you," he said still whispering. Justin came in the barn saying, "You almost done boy? Your mother wants that milk."

"Yes pal," he said with a stern voice while getting up.

"Well get on in the house, I'm getting hungry," Justin said. Ethan and I were walking out of the barn. Just before leaving Justin said, "And maybe next time Katherine, could stay in the house and help Molly you got that boy?"

"Yes pal," he said and we walked up to the house with our baskets and buckets.

"Okay maybe you were right," he said.

"Right about that he doesn't like me?" I teased him. "Yes."

Chapter 8

Ethan and I were sitting waiting for breakfast. All the girls were helping Molly. Eric was down here sitting in one of the chairs playing with the other boys. Molly came in the room with a bowl of gravy and Emma with a basket of biscuits.

"Someone yell for your pal," Molly asked but not to anyone certain.

"I'll do it," Samuel volunteered. Out of all the kids, he's my favorite. However, maybe I shouldn't say that even in my head. Samuel is so easy with things. That one day he wanted me to play with him, and I said a different time. He was alright with it.

"No meat?" Eric asked. Of course, he'd be the one to say that.

"No, no meat. We're running low out in the smoke house," she said.

"Okay let's pray and eat I have a busy day ahead of me," Justin said walking in through the door of the kitchen and the family room. Justin started us off with a prayer, and we began to eat.

"Eric I want you to stay home and rest," Molly said to him. Eric looked up from his plate and stared at her.

"But mama?" he said.

"No buts. I don't want to risk you catching any sickness that could be going around," she was proving her point.

"I'll stay home with him! I know Justin and the girls and the boys are home as well, but they're all doing their things, and I have nothing. I have no reason into going to town," Elizabeth said.

"Okay. So it'll just me, Ethan, and Katherine," she finished. We all finished eating and cleaning up. I went up stairs to go fetch my bag. Ethan followed me in my room.

"Are you going to follow me everywhere?" I asked him.

"Yes, no, maybe?" he answered me. How could you not be sure?" I know he's teasing me.

"C'mon now let's go!" Molly yelled from the bottom of the staircase.

"Coming!" we yelled at the same time. From my room to the stairs, Ethan held my hand. When we got to the barn Ethan got out the horse and the wagon. And we were on our way to town.

...

We were parked at the same place when I first met Ethan. It was just out of town. Ethan went to tie up the horses.

"Here I want you to have some of this," Molly said to me handing me some money.

"Molly, I couldn't. The family needs it more than I do," I tried to explain to her. But she refused.

"I want you to have it. Half of it was to Elizabeth, but she didn't come, and you girls are part of the family." There was nothing that I could say. She was going to win no matter what.

"Thank you."

"Now go buy you something good or even better something you could use," she said. We were all walking to the general store. We walked in, and the town folks were staring at us. I first looked around to see what there was.

Paper they had paper here, and diary's as well! I had enough to get a new diary because I'll be in need of one soon. I grabbed what I need and paid. Molly was talking to one of the other town folks. I was looking around to find Ethan, who was outside talking. He did come in with us, but I guess I was too excited about finding the diaries, I didn't realize that he went back outside. I remembered I have mama's letter with me that I need to mail. The thing is I don't know where the post office is at? I walk outside to ask Ethan.

"E-Ethan," I hesitated. He looked over towards me.

"Yes Katherine?"

"Where's the post office at?" I asked. He pointed the way for me saying to go left.

"Thanks," I said and left him to talk some more. Was he ignoring me? I'm not sure what his deal was? Well, I found the post office right where he pointed to. As I walked in I could smell this nasty smell coming from the clerk. He was a very old man. I'm surprised that isn't the smell of death. I didn't say much to him only gave him my letter to mail it to this address. It was my house, yeah I know my father will see it but the maids always get the mail before he does. After getting done with him, I left as soon as I could to find Ethan. He was still there talking so I went on back in the store to find Molly.

She was finished getting her things. She had some flour and seasonings.

"Well I'm ready if you're ready?"

"Yes," I said. As, we walked out Ethan grabbed the sack of flour for Molly. I only had my bag. The trip back to the house was the same as going to town. We were quite that's the only thing I didn't mention. So what I'm saying is we're home now. We were gone for about half the morning. Molly was starting dinner because that was going to take about another hour. Ethan and I went our separate ways to do things. Molly and I were in the kitchen fixing what she had me to fix.

"July 4th there's family that's coming up to visit," she said.

"You're family?" I asked.

"Yes, they always come up," she said.

"Don't tell the boys but the reason we only had biscuits and gravy for breakfast is so we have enough meat for the holiday. You would think after years of doing this they would know? I think Ethan is smart enough to know I'm just worried about Eric." She had a lot to say about this.

Throughout all of dinner Ethan was staring at me. He was sitting across from me. I would take a bite while looking down at my plate. Then when I look up, he would be staring at me. What is going on through his head?

After dinner was over Ethan came and grabbed my arm. I was about to head up stairs to write in my diary for the day.

"Hey the only reason I didn't say anything to you about the post office was because of the reason of Jacob Wells. He really believes in the whole thing about women can't interrupt when men are talking." He was right about the entire women's situation.

He let's go of my arm after I kept on looking at it giving him a sign that he needs to let it go. I then head up stairs to leave him. Once in my room, I open up my new diary and began to write.

Days later go by…

…

July 4, 1860 afternoon

Dear Diary,

Molly's family is here. Some brought food as well when we all were up early baking. I have one thing to say about her family; I like them. There really heartwarming and out in the open to anything. Maybe that's why Molly was so nice to Elizabeth and me when we first moved in. There are grandparents, aunts, uncials, nephews, nieces, and cousins. Molly has two elderly brothers and three elderly sisters. That makes her the youngest.

I need to be down stairs for the party. I really didn't have much to say or to do. I guess you could say I'm bored. I need to go. That's all I'm just going to say for now, bye.

Love Katherine

…

I left my room to go outside where the party was held at. Outside we had two tables with food. One had our meals, and the other table had pies and cakes. When it was time to eat all of us, older kids ate in the one wagon that was close. The grownups all were seated at a table which one family brought over and the other family was responsible of bringing chairs. And the littler kids all eat on the porch. Before we all prayed one of the men said that we could have as much as we want.

I had a total of two plates and so did Elizabeth. We think the boys are on their third plate by now, but we don't know. After all of us, older kids were finished, we all started walking to the barn. I knew that Samuel and Jeffrey wanted to come and hang out with us but their older cousins said no, which hurt their feelings. I turned around and to stop the boys to say, "Hey, Samuel, Jeffrey." They came up to me as I got down on my knees.

"I know you two want to be with us, but you wouldn't like what we are talking about," I said to them. They just stared at me with sad faces.

"How about I play with you later tonight, deal?" Their faces lit up after I said that.

"You promise?" Samuel asked.

"I never break a promise. Now get over here and give me a big hug!" I said to them as they both tried to squeeze the life out of me.

"Now go get out of here and go play with your cousins who are your own age!" I yelled at them as they ran off to go meet up with their other cousins.

As I turned around I saw one of Ethan's girl cousins staring at me with a dirty look. I don't really know everyone's names and hope not to after seeing hers. A few of the boys not Ethan or Eric were jumping into the family wagon. I went to stand next to Elizabeth in the barn. All a sudden Eric was hooking up Roller and Chester to the wagon, and one of the other boys had a long thing of rope in his hands. Ethan came up to Elizabeth and me with a smile on his face.

"We're all going down by the river to go swimming. Molly allows us because it's part of our fun as well. Would you two like to come?" he asked. I was staring at his brown eyes lost to what he had said. I could see from the corner of my eye that Elizabeth looked at me for one second and then went back to him to say, "We've loved to come."

All of us piled into the wagon, and of course the boys were sitting up front. There were four boys and four girls. This is counting Ethan, Eric, Elizabeth, and me. Rick and Austin were their names. They were brothers. Samantha is the other cousin, and the other cousin is Natalie. Natalie was the one giving me the dirty look. We were pulling up by the party as Molly was coming up to us and was stopping us.

"Be safe. I want you to come home as soon as you're finished, and before sunset. You're cousins have to have time to make it to town, and I have a feeling that a storm is coming."

"Yes mama," Ethan answered her. We were moving again.

"Have fun!" she yelled while waving. I waved back for the fun of it. The ride there was maybe fifteen minutes long. Rick was riding in the back with all of us girls. He jumped out with the rope in his hands and started climbing a tree.

"Hey, make sure that rope is good and tight you here?" yelled out his brother Austin. Both brothers had blond hair. Samantha had brown hair like me, and Natalie's was red hot like her attitude. The boys all started taking off their shirts, but left their pants on. Rick grabbed a hold of the rope and swung out in the water. Eric ran and pushed Austin in along with Ethan. Elizabeth and I were laughing. Samantha toke off her dress and only left on her under dress. She slowly got in the water. I didn't want to get wet, but I was so hot.

"Hey Katherine, Elizabeth, Natalie you coming in?" called out Rick.

"I don't know these girls look like they're scared. You're going to have to chases me to come in," Natalie said. I really don't like her.

"Oh come on its hot out," Rick again. I looked at Elizabeth and without words, we through off our clothes and jumped in the river holding hands screaming. Natalie was still trying to have Rick come and drag her in the water. Again, she gave me a dirty look.

"There you two go!" Rick said. I think he likes Elizabeth, and I, being in the family. All of us were splashing water around at each other. I was having so much fun. Just watching the little waves was amazing. The water was so cold and refreshing. I wasn't hot anymore from after swimming.

After a little horse playing, we all just flouted around talking. Natalie was still up on the shore watching us.

"Rick your girl wants you to bring her in," Austin said.

"Damn it!" Rick yelled. We were far out to the other side of the river. When Rick said damn it Natalie pocked her head up just a bit. I'm not sure if she heard that though?

"Man I'm hungry again," Eric said. Us girls giggled.

"I brought some barbecue, along just in case we got hungry again," Samantha said. We all then started swimming back to the other side of the river. It wasn't that far. We all dried off as much as we could by sitting in the sun.

"Rick you came for me!" Natalie cheered.

"Ah no we all just came to get something to eat," Rick said to her. Her cheering face went blank. We ate again and sat to talk. Samantha and Elizabeth wanted to go back in the water. Rick and Austin did as well. Rick even grabbed Natalie's hand and brought her in. Ethan and I stayed on shore to relax.

"Are you having fun?" he asked.

"Yes the most I've had in ever!" I answered him with a smile. I saw Elizabeth by the tree with the rope tied to it. She was heisting to jump in.

"Oh come on Elizabeth you can do it!" Austin yelled from the water. Eric was sneaking up on her without her knowing.

"Boo!" he scared her as she screamed and punched him in the arm. Ethan and I and everyone else was laughing at that.

"Here let me help you," Eric said as he put his arms around her waist. I gave Ethan a look, and we smiled. She grabbed a hold of the rope, and as he pushed her; she jumped in the water screaming. She was brave.

"Katherine you want to try it?" Eric asked me.

"No thanks!" I yelled back to him. He turned his head to the rope and jumped into the water. After he jumped and made a bigger splash than Elizabeth did. All five of them were splashing water around.

"Did your family ever do anything like this?" Ethan asked.

"No we never got in the mood. My family is stubborn."

"Now I see why you're always stubborn all the time!" he teased.

"Ah I am not!" and I shoved him to the ground. We were both laughing. We got back up to sit and to rearrange our self's.

"So tell me the story about Natalie?" I asked.

"Natalie, well she too is stubborn."

"When she was little she was adapted by Molly's older brother. She's an only child so that is why she wasn't nice to Sam and Jeff," he explained to me.

The sun was coming down. He was beautiful in the sunlight. I wonder if he thinks the same about me. He was explaining some more to me about Natalie. I lost interest after he said she is an only child.

"Do you think we should start heading back? It looks like Molly was right about it going to rain," I explained. He looked at me and got up. I reached out my hand for him to get me up, but he didn't. He yelled out to the crew yelling, "Hey ass holes we need to go!" They all gave out a grunt. Ethan turned around to help me.

"Oh sorry about that," Ethan and I were dry all the way well almost. When we were talking, we had our wet clothes still on drying. We were dry more now than before so we put our clothes on over.

"Katherine you can sit on up front with Ethan," Rick said to me.

"Thanks!" I said to him because I was surprised that he was going to let me. Austin and Eric went to hitch up the horse to the wagon. All three girls were trying to dry themselves with their dresses. And so did Austin and Eric but not with dresses but with their shirts. As I looked back behind me, Natalie gave me another little dirty look. Now I know she doesn't like me, and I really don't care. Fifteen minutes went by for us to get back to the party. All the tables were put up, and the wagons were all hitched up ready to leave.

"Maybe they're all in the house?" Austin said. After Austin said that the family walked out of the house and was all hugging in the grass. We all went in the barn to put the wagon away. While walking back to the house, we all said our last good-byes. I liked Molly's family; they were nice and funny, all except Natalie.

"Well it's time for the family train to leave. See y'all until Thanksgiving I guess?" said one of the uncials. A few of the smaller children came up to Ethan and Eric to say good-bye to them. They got down on their knees to say, "Bye, see y'all in a few months." I thought it was cute. It maybe took five minutes for all the wagons to leave the property.

"They all need to get to town before dark," Molly said to me as all of us were heading inside the house.

"And then what?" I asked.

"Then they all head their sprat way's home."

"Oh I see."

"You four go get some dry clothes on and head to bed early. I don't want anyone sick." Molly yelled at us as we all got in the house.

"Yes mama," said the boys. We started to head up stairs to go change.

Chapter 9

Molly was right about that there was a storm coming. It looks all gloomy outside this morning. I only want to sleep all day if maybe half the day if I'm allowed. My body is sore from swimming yesterday. I hope I'm not getting sick. Elizabeth wasn't in her bed so that means she's down stairs. I heard a knock on my door.

"Katherine," called out a voice. It was a low voice.

"Come in," my voice was a little scratchy. Ethan poked his head in through the door. His hair was a little wet; he must have just come back from being outside. I gave him a smile. I was still sitting in my bed. He came in slowly walking towards me then sitting on the foot of the bed.

"Are you ready to get up?" he asked. Why did he ask, am I the last one to get up? I hope I didn't sleep past breakfast?

"Molly has breakfast ready. I just came from being outside feeding the animals," he said.

"Yes but I don't want to get up," I complained to him.

"Wait here I'll be right back," he said to me then left. Why does he want me to wait up here when Molly has breakfast ready for us? I got up to change for the day. My legs were hurting the most out of all.

Ethan came in through the door with two bowls of hot food in his hands.

"What is this?" I asked him.

"I talked to Molly saying that you weren't feeling your best today, and she said that you could just rest for the day," he said sitting on my bed and then handing me a bowl. It had oatmeal in it.

"I'll stay up here with you as long as you want me too in order to feel better," he said with a smile appearing on his face.

"I feel fine it's just my body hurts," I complained some more.

"Well I can fix that," he said. I was confused on what he was trying to say? I only gave out a little giggle. We then finished eating, and he took my bowl from me and took it down stairs. When he went down stairs, I was thinking some more on what he was saying about I can fix that? Footsteps are coming up. He's up now I need to stop thinking about him. It's not like he can read minds! We were just sitting on the bed a few inches apart from each other.

I, for some reason, was still not comfortable at least being with him. The reason being is the family. We were talking about a lot of different things. After a while, we started to hear some thunder. I started to feel scared.

"Are you okay?" he asked. Why do I look scared?

"No, thunder scares me," I said to him. I must have made a weird move in order for him to ask. The door opens up and here comes along Eric and Elizabeth both sitting on her bed. They both had a suspicious smile on their faces. Ethan was still on the foot of the bed sitting. I'm glad he didn't do anything stupid or he, and I would have been caught.

"Can we help you?" Ethan asked them.

"No we just wanted to check up on Katherine," Eric said.

"Ah Eric how sweet of you, but I'm okay I just feel really tired this morning," I said.

"Well I wanted to check up on you to Katherine," Elizabeth said really quickly.

"I bet you did Elizabeth. You know I'm feeling much better now. I think I want to go down stairs to sit or go out on the porch to feel some fresh air," I said standing up. Ethan stood up as I did.

"That sounds like a good idea or all of us," Ethan said. Eric and Elizabeth were the first two to go out of the room and down the stairs.

Ethan and I followed. I really wanted him to hold my hand all the way down, but I didn't want to be caught by the family. Once down stairs, Molly and the children were found in Molly's bedroom folding a few blankets. When we reached outside to enjoy the crisp clean rainy air, Eric and Elizabeth got to the porch sewing before Ethan, and I could. So we sat down on the cold damp porch step. Ethan let me sit where it was less wet from one of the fence rail blocking the rain.

"Boy if I swam any longer I bet by this morning my arms would have fallen off!" Eric there is making a joke, and it was somewhat funny because it made Elizabeth, and I laugh.

"Girls his arms did fall off this morning because he didn't want to help me feed the animals," Ethan said.

"No, no I did help you with fixing the old fence rail,"

"Eric, what am I to do with you?" Ethan asked him. "I feel the same Ethan!" Eric said to him. Elizabeth goes up from where she was sitting to look out in the west sky to see the clouds. A gush of wind came by through and made us both shiver just a little. Ethan came close to me and well had his arms around me. However, it was okay because I saw Eric get up from the swing to put his arms around Elizabeth.

"That wind will get you if you don't have the right clothing on," Eric just had to say something like that. I mean the clothing part because he probably really wants to get to Elizabeth close someday. The boys eventually pulled away from us to go sit back down where they were sitting at.

"Where is your father at?" I asked.

"He's out in the barn working on things," Ethan answered me.

"He likes to work a lot doesn't he?" I asked another question.

"Well, yeah he does. He's always had said to me that it was his quiet place to be working on a fence rail or um yeah just working," Eric said. "I think he likes it out there in the barn better than just being with his family talking, laughing, and have a good time," he added.

Elizabeth was still standing up just watching the sky. Once in a while you would hear thunder or see lighting.

"You know it's beautiful when the clouds all start to move in a circle all together," Elizabeth said out laud.

"Wait. What did you say?" Ethan asked her, standing up to see.

"The clouds, they're just magnificent how they move together like a form of dance," She said. Ethan didn't say anything. He was thinking and how do I know when he is thinking he has a pause and then says something.

"Shit, that's not any clouds dancing Elizabeth. That's a twister!" Ethan yelled and ran towards the front of the porch. "What," Elizabeth was flabbergasted. Eric, Elizabeth, and I ran behind him then stopped.

"Pal, TWISTER!" Ethan yelled out to his pal who was in the barn working. The wind was picking up faster. Eric opened the front door to warn the ones inside. I looked at Elizabeth whose face was the same as mine. Molly slammed the door right open with the children following her and screamed, "Follow me!" Justin ran out of the barn as we all ran with Molly to the outhouse. Wait the outhouse?

Just pass the outhouse and a few trees lay a wooden door on the muggy ground. Justin and the older boys were trying to open it. The wind wasn't helping much. Once they slammed the door opened we all waited until the younger children to go in first next Molly after that it was us older kids. Elizabeth and I have never been through anything like this ever in our lives. It was okay for us to scream because the younger children were screaming as well. There wasn't much room in the seller. Only a few chairs and some blankets thrown around and some shelves.

"Elizabeth how could you have not known what a twister is," Eric laughed as we all were trying to find our places to sit.

"I'm from the city! How was I to know that it was a twister?" she asked. She then was inside Eric's arms hiding her face. Ethan came to me sat down and wrapped his arms around me. I didn't hide my face in his body because I want it to see the terrier in everybody's eyes. You could hear the roaring of the twister moving across our land destroying our property.

"Mama I'm scared!" Samuel panicked. Molly looked down at her child but didn't answer him. Molly was sitting in the one chair while Emma and Madison were holding each other while sitting in the other chair.

"Samuel I don't want to hear you crying over there. In the matter of fact, I don't want to hear any of you all crying; you got that!" Justin was yelling. He was angry, and I don't think it's the twister that is making him angry but his family.

"Yes pal," the children answered panicky.

After a few minutes the roaring had stopped but later hail came pouring down. Jeffery opened the door to grab a hand full of the hail. It was coin sized. So for us all to be safe we all stayed in the seller for a little longer. Elizabeth and Eric were whispering over where they were sitting. She was looking all concerned.

"Everyone may I please have your attention, if before we may die in this storm," Eric started.

"Oh God Eric we aren't going to die; the twister has long gone past over us," Ethan explained to his ignorant brother of his.

"I just want it to say that in the last few days, I have been courting Elizabeth," Eric finished. Elizabeth's face went red. Ethan was staring at me as I was to him. We were right about them being together.

"I have nothing to say about that son," Justin said. The hail and rain were coming down harder.

"So you're fine with this pal," Eric asked. Justin didn't answer.

"Pal, mama I too have been courting Katherine," Ethan said slowly maybe because he was scared to say. I wasn't sure if he was ready to tell his parents yet about us. We really haven't talked about this at all.

"Now that my son I have a problem with," Justin complained yelling. I stared over towards Ethan, who then moved his arms away from me.

"Pal I don't understand? How could you let Eric and Elizabeth be together but not Katherine and I? I just don't understand? Mama could you say something, please!" Ethan yelled. The girl's faces were looking scared. I'm not sure if it was from the storm or all the yelling that is going on.

"Oh boy's I love you both, and I'm fine with all of this maybe? I don't know I'm not sure about this?" Molly said confusing. The rain was slowing down at this point, but the thunder was still a rumbling.

"I don't get it! Why him and not me? Why?" Ethan asked while yelling. His parents didn't say anything after that.

"I really don't see why pal, mama?" Eric asked still having an arm around Elizabeth.

"Eric I don't want to hear anything from you," Justin yelled at him. The girls couldn't hold it in anymore and started to cry from all the yelling. Justin and Ethan were getting angry with each other while Molly, Eric, Elizabeth was trying to stay out of it.

"I've had enough of this!" Ethan yelled, got up, then slammed the door open. I also got up to watch as he walked away to the house in the rain.

"Ethan, get back here; we're not done discussing this! Ethan!" Justin was yelling after his son. He then shoved me to the side almost into Eric. Eric grabbed my waist as I was falling and then helped me up. I then started walking out of the seller towards the house. The family followed as well. It was getting darker outside to where we couldn't see if the twister had left any damage? Justin's standing in the rain yelling at his son saying, "Boy get back here we're not done talking!" As I walked by him to get to the porch all I heard from him was, "Damn it." I held the door open for the family to come in.

"Is anyone hungry?" Molly asked. I believe she only asked that to get the children's mind onto something different other then what's going on right now.

"No," said all the children. I left to go up stairs to find Ethan. Eric and Elizabeth followed. I don't know how I'm supposed to feel now at this point? I was standing outside his door as he was standing in the middle of his room with his hands covering his face. Eric and Elizabeth were standing on the turning point of our stair case just watching me.

"Ethan," I said calmly walking towards him.

"Katherine," he cried holding his arms out and then holding me tight. The two were starting to come up until there was a noise from the kitchen.

"We got it," Eric cheered. There was yelling going on down stairs. It was Molly yelling at one of the children.

"I'm so sorry about what happened back there in the seller," he apologized.

"It's alright," I said calmly. It was getting darker outside. I left to give him some space. I went to my room to also have my space. A few hours have gone by, and I've just done nothing. I haven't even changed yet into my night gown. Eric came in with Elizabeth and then got under her sheets. I guess they didn't see me? So I left to find Ethan in his room. "Ethan," I called out. He was lying down on his bed. He sat up slowly with a blank face while running his fingers through his hair. I have to admit it though, but I love it when he runs his fingers through his hair. This time it was my turn to sit down at the foot of the bed, his bed. He was quiet. There were only three things we were hearing. One was the thunder outside; two were

Eric and Elizabeth laughing and giggling in her room, and third was the candles flickering or is that my heavy breathing I'm doing? I was feeling nerves and comfortable being with him.

Can you feel that way? Maybe I guess. He stood up and started pacing. I know he's still angry with his father.

"He's up to something," he said.

"Ethan you don't know that," I said to him still just sitting. I was starting to get tired really tired, but I don't think he's tired though. I didn't want to go in my room to sleep when Eric and Elizabeth are in there snuggled up.

"Or maybe he's going mad and, and he doesn't know whose he's talking to anymore," he went on. I haven't said anything yet to tell him that I still care for what he is saying.

I stood up and got personally close with him and raised my voice, "Ethan maybe this time he just got mad at you, but deep down, inside, he still loves you."

"Katherine that's not it," he said. Okay I give up now!

"He doesn't love me. He never did and he never will," he said raising his voice. We weren't yelling but only raising our voices. At this time, we really weren't sure if the children were even upstairs?

"Yes Ethan," I said.

"Yes Katherine!" he paused and turned away from me and steadily turned his head my way. "You just don't get it," he said little by little. I wonder if his throat hurts or not? I was thinking back to when Elizabeth, and I were at home. How father wanted us to marry those older men. I now feel the same way as Ethan is with his father.

"And you wouldn't have any thought to what had happened between me and my father?" I said angrily and yanked him to face my way. I narrowed my eyes.

"He kicked me out, crying out loud! And On that day I thought he didn't love me, but I know, deep down, inside he still does." Or maybe it's not true after all, I don't know?

"Oh Katherine," Oh Katherine was all he could say at this point? He turned around again to stare out of the window. He couldn't see much for all he would be staring at would just be darkness. I went to sit back down. I yawned and then just lay down on top of his blankets. I had my eyes open to watch him. Should I, however, care at this point? Yes. No. Maybe I don't know? He turned around and slowly came to the bed. He then kneeled down and grabbed my hand.

"Would you like to sleep with me here? Please Katherine," he whispered. There was no way I wasn't going to say no!

"Yes please!" and then I started crying. I moved forward so he could get behind me. We pulled out the blankets, so we could get under them.

"Katherine I'm sorry for making you cry," he apologized.

"I'm sorry that I can't hold it in," I apologized to him.

At this point, my tears were finishing falling down. Ethan was leaning in closer towards me. He had me wrapped up in him holding me. We both were closing our eyes to start kissing. He next moved his one hand under my head and then all over my body. This night was the first night I would be sleeping with Ethan Lee, but only just sleeping no intimacy!

Chapter 10

Ever since last night was the first time in the month and a half Elizabeth, and I have lived here that I remembered our lie. I have nothing else to say about that but only that I am thankful for this wonderful family to take us under their wing. I'm outside sitting on the ground watching Molly hang up the laundry. She didn't need my help but only wanted my company. Today is a beautiful sunny day. The twister we had yesterday didn't leave any damage but only left a few broken-down limbs from our trees. This morning during breakfast Justin wanted Eric and Ethan to help pick up the limbs. I knew Ethan didn't want to do anything with his father, but he knew he had to do it for the family.

It seems like it's been forever since I've seen the sun. I can feel the warm air touching my face. It's like the same genial feeling that Ethan gives me when he's touching me. Ethan is my sun. Molly was almost finished with the laundry. I would glimpse back behind me to watch the men. They weren't doing so well. It looks like Ethan is still arguing with Justin. And Justin is not allowing us to be together.

"Molly, may I ask you a question?"

"Yes darling."

"Well I've already asked Ethan, but I want to hear it from you," I explained to her pretty quickly.

"Well go ahead ask away!" she cheered not knowing what I am to ask her.

"Could you tell me about how your family is the way it is? How most of your children aren't related to most of the others?" I kept asking.

"Katherine slow down I'll answer them all," she said turning around to see me.

"But not here, follow me," she added and started walking towards the apple trees. I got up and followed her. We then sat down on the grass under the tree limbs. Molly was fluffing out her dress as I did as well.

"Let's see, where, do I begin?" she started to say.

"I married David Janes back in 1845 and at the end of that year I was expecting. David died later that next summer from an illness still to this day I don't know what from? That summer in 1846, I gave birth to Emma and Marty."

Hearing it from Molly, it's different from the last time I heard it from Ethan.

"A year later, I married Justin, but since it was my second wedding I kept my madden name. That same year I adopted Eric and Ethan, who at the time were five years old. Late in 1848 I had Savanna. And also in that year I found Madison on my front porch with a note in the basket she was in. Her mother knew who Justin was and said he was the father."

This was different than what I was told by Ethan.

"On our wedding night, he got so drunk that he vanished for a few hours. He was with her, who still to this day we all don't know who she is. Even Justin doesn't remember what she looks like."

I couldn't imagine the questions Madison has always wanted to ask.

"And last in 1857 we adopted Samuel and Jeffrey, who at the time were three years old."

That's a family story you should never forget. I think she's done telling me her story but is just sitting here looking up to the sky. I think she maybe wants to be alone.

...

I'm just relaxing on my bed staring up at the ceiling. The house is quiet, too quiet? Everybody's outside enjoying the fresh air. I think I want to write in my diary, but I don't know where I left it at last? I got up to look under the bed.

"Wait, what's this I found?" I said out loud. It was that wooden box I found a few weeks ago. I didn't have much time to look at it last time. I believed Ethan was coming up stairs that day to get me. Well, I'm alone now. I stood up to sit on my bed. I blow off the dust that the box was collecting. I could only make out one word that said *Molly*?

I couldn't understand why the box had Molly's name engraved on the top of it, and why was it under Savanna's bed before I took it over? It was clearly Molly's box not Savanna's. I slowly slid my fingers over the top of the lid to feel the engraved name. It was so perfect I thought. There wasn't a lock holding it shut so that made it easy for me to look inside it. I just hope I'm not being too nosey?

I opened the lid to see inside. There were lots and lots of old notes. Maybe love note? I got them all out to look at each one at a time. After a while, I found out that some were pomes, songs, love, and hateful notes. I read each one. I felt guilty after I got finished. She wrote songs, and love and loathsome notes about her family. The love notes were about her children, and the hateful notes were about her husband's. Does she not love her husband Justin? I mean if I was married to him; I wouldn't be either.

That reminds me of the time when Elizabeth, and our fathers were going to have us get married to two older men whom we didn't know a thing about. Ha that is a funny story just between me! I'm being sarcastic! This is bad; I think Eric's getting to me! Damn! This seems simple enough to write little good and bad things about your family. I would do this if I got married to who loves me for me and not money no matter how rich or poor we were. I have not yet thought about marriage with Ethan. I really don't want to think about that right now.

Before putting back all the notes I stared into the wooden box to see inside. Only just on the bottom of the box there was some cloth laying. There were nails holding it down. The color was only brown; I would have gone with blue. I notice that there were a few pieces of paper under the cloth. I had to rip part of the cloth to get them out to read them. I feel a little terrible that I'm reading these notes that Molly wrote from her good and dreadful times in her past.

There were two papers. The first one read, "Jake and Molly Tyler." These were not David and Tyler isn't her last name either? The other paper had a name on it saying, "Abigail Molly Tyler." Then it said my first born. Now I'm getting confused? Molly's two first born children were Marty and Emma.

I put the papers back with the rest of the papers accepted the two other. I shoved the box back under the bed and walked out of the room. Down stares was quiet. Everyone must still be outside. Scenes I didn't really want anyone seeing what I had in my hand, I hide my hands behind my back. I walk outside to find Molly, who was still out by the apple trees staring off into space. I slowly would walk to her.

"Molly," I stared to say clenching my fist, but not crumbling up the papers.

"Kath…" Before she could even get my name out, I interrupted her.

"Molly I want the truth!" She stood up brushed the dirt off her dress and stared deep into my eyes.

"The truth?" she said calmly. It's like she already knows what I'm about to ask her.

"Who are these people?" I showed her the names on the papers. She looked down at them then back at me.

"Where did you find these?" she whispered while yanking the papers out of my hands.

"Molly," I started to say. "I found them in a wooden box under my bed why?"

"These are to my privet box that I had hidden away for a long time!" she panicked. She would just look down at her hands and then run her fingers through her curly hair.

"Molly," I said calmly once when she looked up at me.

"How much do you know? How much do you know?!" She started to shout. I just stood there with my mouth open. I would only move my eyes to see if anyone was hearing or staring over at us. I couldn't see much.

"Molly I only know as much as you told me last and that's it, nothing else!" I raised my voice as I grabbed her wrist, so she could see me explaining it to her. She didn't know what to do, and then she didn't know what to say. I was staring into her eyes.

"I just want to know?" I asked calmly. She gave me a dead stare. After that she started walking past me then grabbed my wrist.

"Follow me…" she said as she was taking me to where she wanted to go.

"Molly, where are we going?" I tried asking her. She didn't answer. Luckily, we were nowhere to be seen by the family.

After a while, of walking we were off our property and into the woods. We stopped out of nowhere with silence.

"Tell me child what do you see around you?" she asked with a stern voice. I looked around to see. All there was are just trees and ground.

"What am I to be looking at Molly?" I panicked.

"This is where my first husband Jake, and my first-born child are buried at."

There was silence again. I looked around one more time to find a cross, but nothing. Molly bent down by a tree to put her hand on it. There was no wooden cross or a tombstone. There where she was two medium-sized stones that she turned around after she got back up. They both had something engraved on them. The first one revealed Jake Tyler 1826-1844. And the second one revealed Abigail Tyler 1844-1844.

"Jake and Abigail Tyler," I whispered to myself.

"No one knows about this," she said almost crying. I wasn't sure who she meant by no one?

"Who is no one?"

"My family," she cried turning her head to face me.

"Even Eric and Ethan don't know about it either?" I asked.

"Yes they too. They still believe David is, however, my first husband even though they never knew the man."

I wanted to ask her how they both died, but didn't want to upset her with her having to live the memory again. I'm such a fuel to be doing this, but here I go, "How did they die?" She stared over at me with both of her arms grabbing each other. Tears were falling down her face as it was getting red by her cheeks.

"I knew you were going to ask," she said whipping away the tears. She sighed.

"Jake was seventeen and I was sixteen when we got married in 1843. By winter that year we knew we were expecting. By May of 1844, we had terrible storms. One-night lighting struck the barn, and Jake ran out to save the animals. I was waiting on the porch praying to God for that he is to be saved. After a while, I knew something was wrong. The back of the barn was half falling down, and most of the rain took out the fire. However, Jake was nowhere to be seen. I couldn't run to go find him, but I did find him." She stopped to take a breath and then to wipe some more tears away.

"I found him lying on the ground with burn marks all over him. He wasn't breathing. I knew it wasn't safe for me to be in the barn with smoke everywhere, but I managed to get him out. We were too far away for me to call for help, and I didn't know where any of our horses had gone. So I laid beside him all night just praying that God would bring him back to me." She fell to the ground, and I ran to her to hold her.

"By morning, I knew he was gone. We had his funeral a few days later right here where we are. And on June 5th I had his daughter Abigail, who soon passed. I had my older sisters and my mama with me that morning just trying to comfort me. Once when I could walk we had her buried next to her father. I couldn't talk to anyone. I had my sisters and some of their family living with me. And seeing them with their husbands and children made it even harder for me. I would cry every night. After a while, I couldn't eat or sleep. Afterwards, I started to write out my feelings. I love my family so much, but I miss this family too." She buried her head on to her knees. I didn't know what do stay or leave her be?

"Where is the box?" she asked.

"In my room, how or why was it there to begin with?" I asked.

"I, I don't know why. Maybe Savanna or Madison found it under my bed to use to play with it; I don't know?" she cried some more.

"I just hope they didn't read my notes?"

"Can they read?" I asked her. She looked up at me and nodded her head no.

"Just remember, this Katherine," she started to say.

"Love comes through time," she said and then buried her head into her arms. After a while, I thought some more about leaving her; I'm not sure. I decided to let her be by her love and child. I thought it was awkward when I was trying to leave. I mean all I did was just get up and started walking back home. I was getting closer to the barn. I also have been crying. What if Ethan saw me and then starts asking me question? Maybe I'll say that I was thinking of my family, and it really got to me. Yeah. Now to think about it, I really do miss my family. How my father doesn't want to listen

to what I have to say, and how mama would comfort me when I was having a bad day. I truly miss my family!

I decided not to stop by the barn. I might make a fuel of myself if Justin saw me crying. So I'm walking fast as I could. However, I make the mistake of looking to my right and watching Ethan stare at me.

"Katherine what is it!" he yells stopping what he was doing. I started to run from him by running behind the barn.

"Wait, hold on!" he yells after me. From what I saw the men were cutting and chopping the broken-down lambs, from the storm and are going to make it fire wood. I stopped and fell on my butt with my back against the wall to the barn.

"Katherine," he called out and then sat down next to me just holding me.

"What happened? What's wrong?" he asked. The next thing that was going through my mind was the first lie I told him. If I tell him this next lie, it'll be two lies since I've met him. However, this second one would not matter as much.

"It's my family; I just really miss them!" I cried.

"Your fine though I got you," he said calmly and then kissed the top of my head. I have no clue to what time it is? I like this part because I get to cry out whatever I want to, and Ethan is there to comfort me.

…

Supper was quiet tonight. We just had a plain simple meal together. After eating Ethan grabbed my arm and took me up to his room. While walking up stairs I would watch Justin giving a mean stare at us. Once in his room, we sat down on the bed and started getting closer by the face. Eye's half way closed.

"Are you okay?" he stopped and asked. Who stops at the beginning of a kiss to ask a question? Oh wait, we do!

"Yes I'm fine," I answered him. "Why you ask?"

"Well during supper, you haven't said a thing," he said moving his hand down my cheek while moving some hair out of the way. After a while, of living here I have forgotten to brush my hair a few times. Perhaps it wasn't quiet during supper, maybe I was thinking too hard about different things and just blocked out everyone.

"How about you go get dressed for bed, and we'll just stay in here until we fall asleep," he said. I nodded and got up to go fetch my nightgown. Once in my room, I changed out of my dirty dress and brushed my hair. I washed my face to clear my mine. What is wrong with me? I'm not sure if it's from Molly's story or that I really only miss my mama? I believe it's both. I left the room to meet up with Ethan in his room. As I walk in I see him lying on his bed. Our relationship just started, and I don't think we're ready for the other stuff to come.

He stood up quick. He hasn't gotten dressed. I think he likes to wait so that I would watch him take off his shirt. Ethan removes his suspenders and slowly taking off his shirt. I sat down to make faces at him. He would laugh.

"You know I have fun with you!" he said sitting down. Well, that's nice to know?

"Really," I asked.

"Yes!" he smiled. We lean in closer to kiss. Next we got under the coverts and just talked. Next to his lips which I love the most I really love his brown eyes and how he has freckles lying on top of his cheeks right under them.

Love comes through time I thought.

Chapter 11

Katherine?

Katherine?

I believe that my name is being called out but by whom? I slowly opened my eyes. Ethan's head was close to mine with his mouth open. The door slowly opened, and Molly's head came popping in.

"Oh lord!" she yelled out then slamming the door closed. Ethan sat up scared as I did as well. Molly came in.

"Ethan get out of that bed, you here?" she screamed.

"Mama no!" he yelled.

"Ethan! You have never said no to me ever before!"

"Mama we were only sleeping nothing else!" he tried explaining to her.

"Sleeping? There will not be any sleeping together until after marriage!"

"Mama it's not like that!" he tried to explain to her.

"Katherine I need you. So will you come with me?" she asked. Ethan climbed over me.

"Mama out, out!" he yelled pushing her out of the room.

"Ethan," she yelled at him. I stood up out of bed.

"OUT!" he yelled slamming the door closed then locking it. "Damn it," he whispered. Right when he yelled out and slammed the door at the same time I jumped. Molly was knocking on the door trying to get our attention but is failing. Ethan walked over to the window to look outside. I came in behind him to rub his back and then to hug him.

"Whatever the reason is that she needs you; it can wait. I want you this morning before I start my chores," he finally calmed down then turned around to hold his hands by my waist.

"Yes but Ethan what if it was really important?" I asked. He covered my mouth by his finger to shut me up.

"Shh I just want you right now," he whispered. I'm melting inside. My heart almost skipped a beat! Okay Katherine just breathe.

"Ethan unlock this door right now!" Molly yelled. I turned around. However, before that, Ethan stopped me and just held me tight.

"Ethan she really needs me," I started to worry.

"No stay here with me. Just stay," he whispered in my ear. I ran my fingers through his hair. Our lips started to touch. He embraced me, and we fell on his bed.

In the front of my nightgown, it was buttoned up. He slowly unbutton a few and then steadily started kissing down my neck. I started to tingle everywhere. Then suddenly we heard Eric came out of Elizabeth's room. Molly screamed but not a scared scream as Eric tried coming in the room but failed because the door was locked. Ethan looked up at me, and we both started to laugh.

"Ethan you better open this door!" he yelled.

"No Eric!" he said. We would still hear Molly yelling in the background. Now at this point, I believe Molly finally left us older kids be in the morning.

Eric then ran into the door opening it up with what strength he has. Ethan and I sat up as I hurried to cover myself up. Ethan hurried to try to help. Eric is standing there with his paint's unbutton and his shirt covering up his waist! Elizabeth then ran in with her nightgown half button down like mine. Both of their hairs were all in a mess.

"What are you two doing in here?" he asked. Eric and Elizabeth stared at each other then back at us.

"Well, we heard mama yelling at you two, and so I hurried to come over here so she wouldn't have seen me with Elizabeth," Eric said.

"Oh. And button your paints back up," Ethan laughed.

"We're all going to be in trouble," Elizabeth said.

"Yes, yes we are," Ethan said, shaking his hair. Eric finally got dressed in what he was sleeping in an Elizabeth, and I finally button up our nightgowns. This has been a weird morning.

...

By dinner time, Molly and Justin sat us down by the table for a talk. Molly and Justin were walking around.

"Okay children we fully understand that you want to sleep with whom you love," Molly started. "But Justin and I didn't think it would happen this fast?"

"Mama please?" Ethan tried to say something until, "No Ethan not now," by Molly.

"Boy, you should just shut the hell up for not following the rules with your mother!" Justin yelled while pointing his dirty figure at him.

"I mean you have no brain in there. If there was a wagon coming your way you'd get hit!" Justin laughed not knowing that Ethan saved my life from a wagon coming my way.

"I mean you don't listen to your mama, and you especially don't listen to me when I clearly said you cannot court Katherine," he kept on going.

"You are the dumbest and stupidest boy I have ever seen. You're lousy with your work and when taking care for the animals. I'm surprised that you haven't killed them yet if it wasn't for me and Eric." Okay now he's gone too far.

"Justin stop it. Okay just stop it before someone gets hurt!" Molly yelled.

"Boy down in George we would hit our slaves. However, you're my stepson."

Ethan stood up as his chair fell back behind him and clinched his fist.

"Well, you see I'll only be your stepson," he said angry.

"No, no you aren't," Justin started to laugh and then said, "And the next thing next to your dumbness and stupidity and your dumb girl you're courting!"

And then right there was where it happened Ethan punched his father in the nose. My heart was going a thousand times as fast. We all gasped as Justin fell to the floor with a bleeding lip and nose. Ethan stood over him.

"She is not dumb! She is smart and is smarter than you'll ever be! I LOVE HER!" he cried and just left the room to go outside. He slammed the door harder than what it was this morning. Molly ran over to Justin and started helping him by grabbing his arm as he said to her, "No Molly I'm fine just go get that boy of yours."

"Go to hell Justin!" she said leaving him be there lying on the floor. I was just sitting there staring at him as he was staring at me. There were so many hands on my back and my arms and my knees. Molly, Eric, and Elizabeth were trying to talk to me but all I could hear was, "I love her," in his voice just repeating in my mine. I stood up maybe called out Ethan's name and ran outside to find him.

"Ethan!" I yelled as he turned around in the middle of the drive. I ran to him as he ran to me. We wrapped our arms around each other and then kissed.

"That was the bravest thing anyone has ever done for me!" we kissed again.

"I love you," I whispered to him with both of our foreheads touching one another's.

"Let's run away," he whispered. I had to think this over. I've already ran away once I'm not sure if I want to do it a second time?

"But your family is here," I whispered. At this point, we're just whispering or talking softly. He was moving his hands down my arms slowly and then holding my hands outward.

"Well then let's just get away for the night."

"Ethan we don't have any money," I complained. He appeared a smile on his face.

"You see my girl; I've been putting back some money ever since I was little. I have enough for one or two nights," he said. I leaned in close to his ear and whispered, "Where is it."

"In my room, there is a chest. In that, chest is a box. You'll see it because it's the only box in there. Just grab it and a few clothes for the both of us. However, be sneaky and careful. I'll go hook up the wagon," he whispered to me when I had my eyes closed trying to imagine all of this.

I opened my eyes and turned around. As soon as I did that I could see Eric and Elizabeth watching us from inside. Once inside they came at me one by one. I ignored them and just walked on through. I went to Ethan's room first. I scrambled around to find the chest to grab the box of money. Then I went looking through his dresser for some of his clothes. Next I moved to my room to put all of our things together in one bag. I didn't know how I was going to get through down stares without being seen? Right now, I'm all about taking any chance to be with Ethan.

I thought it over wants when I get down stares I'll stop once and say what comes at the top of my head and walk out with no other words and run to Ethan. So far, so good, I thought.

"Katherine stop, wait, look at me!" This time I finally hear Elizabeth once when I got down stairs.

"What are you doing? What are you both doing?" she asked. She basically had me pinned up. I know they can see the bag, but yet they haven't questioned that.

"Elizabeth let me go! We know what we're doing!" I yelled and ran passed her and the others. Ethan was out by the road. Once outside I ran to him. I through the bag in the back and ran to him as he helped me up quickly. I looked back behind us to see Eric and Elizabeth watching us leave.

"Good-bye we love you. We'll be back soon!" I yelled as Ethan and I waved at them.

Just now, I thought of whether Justin got on one of the other horses and started chasing us or Eric. However, Justin was hurt, and Eric wouldn't think of anything like that until tonight if maybe. No Eric is really smart he just likes to act dumb, so we could all laugh at him. Right now, it's just a steady ride. Ethan put his arm around me and kissed the top of my head.

"Are you sure about this?" I asked him.

"Yes. Besides we're only going to be gone for two days," he said and smiled.

"It's going to be dark before we get there. Are you ready for that?" I asked.

"As long as I got you, I'm ready for anything to come!"

"You know you don't have to act all tough just because you through one at Justin," I said.

He then started to move his arm away from me. I know it was what I said but still.

"Katherine didn't you hear what he was saying about me, about us?"

"Yes Ethan I did hear him," I answered him. He then moved my head close to his and started to say, "Listen, I would do whatever it takes to protect you."

"You would?" I smiled.

"Yes."

...

Right when we got to Greenfield, it became nightfall. Ethan parked the wagon behind the Inn building where all the wagons can be parked at for the night. He jumped out first then helped me down. He ran to the back to grab our bag. He grabbed my hand, and we started walking to find the front door. Once inside we checked in and put our one bag away lying on the bed.

"They're still serving supper are you hungry?" he asked.

"Yes I am," I answered. We walked out of the room. Ethan locked the door so no one could break in. He held his hand against my back just right above where my butt is. It's in the same position from the last time he had it there on the first day we met after he saved me.

Once in the dining room, we sat down and our waiter came by to ask what we'll be having.

"Just give us the special for the night," he said and the waiter left.

"This is nice for once," he smiled staring at me. It was only us and two other tables here tonight in the dining room.

"Yes it is," I laughed. It didn't take long for our meals to come since they made it a while ago. We had each slice of turkey with some mashed potatoes and a roll. We eat a few bites first before talking some more. However, instead, we didn't talk and just finished eating.

After we were done eating we sat there staring into each other's eyes. Or so I believe that is what we are doing? Ethan got up and stood by my side as I sat there.

"Stay here I'll be right back to pay," he whispered. He forgot the money in the room from after paying the clerk for our room. It didn't take him long to get here. He paid the cheek and laid a tip down, and then we left to go to our room.

Once in our room Ethan locked the door behind him. I walked up to him to kiss him. We haven't stopped. We were really into it. We slowly started to take our clothes off standing there. While moving backward to the bed his shirt fell to the ground. We laid there breathing heavily gazing into each other's eyes.

"Are you ready for this?" he asked.

"No I'm not," I sigh. We sat up and stared at the ground.

"It's okay I wasn't sure if you were wanting too or not. I was only thinking of now." He got down on his knees and held my hands and said, "Katherine we can put that to aside," he said.

"Okay," I whispered. He leaned up on his knees to kiss me.

We then got up to get dressed. We were comfortable to get dressed in front of each other. I grabbed my brush to brush my hair on the bed. Ethan came up behind me slowly kissing down my neck and running his hand down my tangled hair. All we heard was us breathing. Then we sat back under the blankets as Ethan was on top of me. He looked at me and leaned in order to kiss my lips. I could taste his taste, and I liked it. He then embraced me, and that was how the rest of the night went on.

...

I awoke feeling alive. Late at night I woke up once to remember where I was at and who I was with. I felt more comfortable to sleep with Ethan. However, as I am getting up and getting dressed, I find myself lonely. And again being in an Inn I am left to be in the room alone in the morning. Suddenly, the door opens up and Ethan came through it walking up to the bed with something in his hands.

"Moring how'd you sleep?" he asked sitting next to me.

"Great, even though our bed beck home is more comfortable than this one."

"Here take it," he said handing me a muffin with a smile.

"Thank you," I took a bite into the muffin. It was warm inside.

"I hid them from the workers. I didn't want them to see me take them out of the dining room!" he laughed.

"Ha wow," I smiled. I believe this is all we're eating this morning?

"I was thinking that we should go out for a picnic in the woods."

"A picnic," I said.

"Yes."

"Ethan, what about the food?"

"I'll deal with it," he said.

"And a basket?"

"Like I said I'll deal with it. Don't you worry?"

"Okay," I murmured.

Around dinner time Ethan went to do whatever it was that he has in plain for the evening. He had me waiting outside. I was leaning against the rail where you would tie up your horse. I was really outside of the general store while Ethan was inside. He comes out of the door holding a brand-new basket saying, "Just one more stop, and we'll be on our way. So if you won't mind waiting here."

And he just left me without finishing his sentence. After maybe five minutes he came back to me.

"You ready," he asked although if he asked himself that question before he had me wait outside of town, he would have said no!

"Yes," I smiled. During the walk to where he wanted us to go, we stayed quiet. We were really saving up our long conversation for when we are eating.

"This seems decent right here!" he said just stopping where he felt was a good spot to eat. He sat the basket down and opened it up. He then pulled out a small blanket and laid it on the ground. He sat down and handed me his hand too so I could sit next to him.

"So what did you bring?" I asked waiting to see what he brought me.

"Close your eyes and wait until I say you can open them!" he smiled. So I closed my eyes. It didn't take long for him to do whatever it is that he is doing.

"Okay you can open your eyes!" he said slowly but happy. I opened my eyes to find a plate filled with bread and ham!

"How," I started to say.

"How I could afford all of this, or how did I get all of this?"

"Um, both," I smiled.

"Maybe how I got it doesn't matter," he said. It's like he doesn't want to tell me. We then started to eat.

After a while, we decided to lie down to rest. Then we went for a walk because he had to pee! I told him I was going to go in the bushes after he cheeked for anything that was poisons. We sat down by a tree at opposed ends getting to know each other better or not. What I'm thinking about is bringing up the conversation about the family.

"What are we going to do tomorrow?"

"I'm not sure on what you are asking me?" he said confused.

"I mean your family." I like to get straight to the point. He hasn't said anything yet.

"Ethan?" I called out, but still no answers.

"Ethan!"

"Katherine, hush! There's a bear over by those trees!" he whispered.

"What I don't hear a bear," I started to say then leaning over to see him and to find him not there.

I stood up quick and panicked. I started to hear some footsteps, but I wasn't sure if it was the bears or not. I stood by the tree with my back against the trunk of it. I looked over to my right once more. There was no bear or Ethan.

"Watch out!" Ethan grabbing my waist knocking us down scaring me! I screamed of course. As we fell down he landed on me laughing.

"Ethan!" I yelled as we fell. "Ethan what about the bear?" I whispered.

"Oh I made the whole thing up, but you should have seen your face!" he laughed.

"Ethan is this your way of having fun!" I yelled at him. His smile vanished.

"Why did I scare you?" he asked. He was lying on top of me. I mean it's not like it's our first time. Ha there's Eric getting to me again.

"Are you angry?" he asked again.

"Yes you scared me and yes; I am angry!" I raised my voice. I forced him to get off of me.

"Get off of me" I said pushing him to the side. After that I started walking back to town.

"Oh come on Katherine! It was only a joke! Where are you going?" he yelled as I didn't turn around. I'm not mad at him to where it's more of me being embarrassed. He made the whole thing up by faking a bear.

"I'm going home!" I yelled.

"Well you're going the wrong way!" I stopped but didn't turn around because I just know he's going to say something else. I heard him walking up to me.

"And how do you know I'm going the wrong way?" I asked angrily then turning around to see his face.

"I just know and besides you're not from around here, I am," he said manly.

"Then tell me where to go, and I'll go!" I yelled and said, "Or how about the damn bear should tell me where to go!"

"Are you mad at me for just having some fun with you," he raised his voice.

"Yes I'm mad. You shouldn't have done something like that." I said sarcastically.

"I was just having some fun."

"Fun or just wanting to embarrass me," I said and then turning around again crossing my arms.

He came up behind me. I turned my head just a bit as his arms moved all around my shoulders and sides.

"Katherine I didn't mean to embarrass you. I only meant to make memories with you."

"I'm sorry," he whispered but no kiss not even on my ear or neck. He had his hand covering my heart, and I had my hand covering it as well.

...

Night.

We're in our room standing on our knees on the bed.

Kissing. Breathing. Thinking?

I'm still embarrassed from earlier. However, to think about it, it gave me the passion I have now with him. What we're doing and what we're saying. Who knows what we're going to do tonight? Because I'm not sure and maybe he doesn't either. Tonight we both didn't feel like eating or talking much.

I think I give in too easy? Or I forgive too easy? I defiantly forgive way too much especially with him. Let me see we've had maybe three fights. I jerked up a tad. His left hand made it down south to far by my butt. I had to move it back up. And as I was doing that I was thinking of all of our past fights.

Our first one started with the night; he almost didn't kiss me, then the one right before our first kiss. That night after the twister was our third and the one we had earlier was our fourth.

Like what Molly said to me love comes through time.

Love comes through time.
Love comes through time.
Love comes through time I thought.

And sleep comes as we both get under the coverts.

Dream. Dreaming is the only other place besides my diary, I can escape from anything that has been going on around me. Is this love? Is this love that we have between us? Now being with Ethan my dreams have been becoming nightmares to where if we are together or not. To where he's only faking it all. To where he knows about my lie, and he wants in on *my* money.

These have been the different things I have been dreaming about. About us. My eyes are getting heavy as Ethan moves his arm over me holding me in bed.

I think for one last time before falling to sleep.

Love comes through time.

Chapter 12

Morning. The sun shining through the opening of the currents and the smell of coffee and bad morning breath is what woke me up. Ethan was staring at me as we both were still lying down under the coverts. We got out of bed and changed for the day. Then we ate and later packed our one bag to leave. During the whole way home we didn't talk. My heart has been pounding the way back home. I'm worried for what will happen.

"Have you ever driven a wagon before?" Ethan asked. I looked over towards his way with a half smile.

"No why you ask?"

"Oh I was just wondering. Would you like for me to teach you?" he asked. I had to think about this?

"Sure why not!" I chuckled. He then moved his arm around me and hugged me with a bright smile on his face. We were only a few feet away from his drive. Once pulling in all the children were outside playing.

They came running up to the wagon greeting us. Ethan stopped the wagon and jumped out. Then he helped me down by reaching his hand.

"Katherine, Ethan we thought you left us for good!" Savanna cried. She came in through Ethan and I and hugged my waist. Emma and Jeffery did the same with Ethan. Samuel, Madison, and Marty staid back and waited.

"Where's mama and pal at?" Ethan asked. The children just stared at each other with blank faces on them.

"Pal's out in the fields working with Eric and Mama's inside with Elizabeth," Marty said. Ethan grabbed my fingers slowly and reached farther up onto my hand.

Ethan leaned in close and whispered, "Let's get our things in the house, and we'll deal with everything in a moment." We didn't look at each other then I nodded. Ethan took a step back to go get the bag. He knelled down next to Jeffery and asked, "Can you watch out for mama and pal?" Jeffery didn't understand why his big brother asked him that. Ethan nodded his head then Jeffery later followed his nod.

Ethan then stood up and grabbed my hand, and we started walking in the house after Jeffery.

"Follow me. Don't stop for Molly or Elizabeth you hear?" he asked stopping before he evens open the front door. I nodded. We went inside the house passing Molly's room.

"Ethan?" Molly called out.

"Katherine?" Elizabeth did the same. However, Ethan and I didn't stop. We just ran on through the house to his room. The children stopped by Molly's room, so they wouldn't come chancing us. Ethan doesn't have any of this planned out. He's just going with what he can with what he has.

Once in his room he through our bag on the floor and locked the door. I was standing there with my eyes wide open watching him with his head leaning against the front of the door. He turned around and came close.

"Now what?" I asked then he pressed his finger up against my lips.

"I'm not sure?" Then he took a step back and grabbed my hand once more. He unlocked the door, and we ran down the stairs. Before we could even step onto the hard wood floor Molly was there standing with her arms by her waist.

"Mama I'm so glad to see you!" Ethan cheered and tried to hug her. Molly just stood there not even hugging back until, "Oh Ethan I can't stay mad at you." Elizabeth came up to me from the side, and we hugged.

"Katherine," she whispered in my ear.

"Yes Elizabeth?" I whispered back.

"Nothing I just wanted to say your name." We then let it go of each other. I looked over towards Molly to see her smiling at me.

"How are you Katherine?" she asked walking towards me still smiling.

"I'm great!" We all walked into the kitchen because Molly had to stir the stew. Elizabeth was looking out the window and started to say, "Oh I just saw Eric walking toward the barn I'll go and get him!"

"Elizabeth wait," Molly raised her voice stopping her just before she almost got out through the door.

"Don't mention anything about Ethan and Katherine getting here now if Justin is in there too," she said waiving the hot spoon around. Elizabeth nodded and walked out slowly.

"I think I frightened the poor girl!" Molly chuckled. Ethan and I were standing next to each other with our arms around one another. The children were back outside playing as I could see through the window. Suddenly, the front door swings open and Eric comes walking in with wide-open arms.

"You two!" he said excitedly hugging us both at the same time. Eric stepped back and held Elizabeth's hand.

"Let's talk in the other room," Ethan said. All four of us kids walked in the one room where the first family fight started as I know of? We all sat down.

"So how's pal?" Ethan asked.

"He's fine I'd say," Eric looked concerned.

"Is he still mad at us? I mean me?" I looked over at him and stared to say, "Ethan he can't just be furious only at you. He possibly has to be angry with me as well."

"No Katherine it's just me!" He took my hand and held it over the table. I yanked it right out.

"He hasn't said much." Eric added as he glanced over at Elizabeth.

"Oh shut up Eric! Katherine, Ethan he has not stopped once talking about you two," Elizabeth interrupted Eric.

"God Eric why couldn't you just say so instead of lying to my face!" Ethan stood up. Eric was speechless.

"Ethan sit down your pal is coming!" Molly yelled from the kitchen. However, Ethan did not sit down. The door swings open and walking through it was Justin. He was covered with dirt and sweat.

"Oh I see you're finally home," He said walking into the dining room.

"Yes pal I am. Would you like for me to do anything outside for you," Ethan added hoping to make things any better? I was still sitting down watching them have a conversation.

"In the matter of fact I do. You could go and finish maintaining the fields for the rest of the evening," he smiled. Justin only wants him to work hard and by himself.

"Yes sir," he said. Then Ethan sat down next to me.

"What are you doing boy?" Justin asked.

"I'm waiting for mama to get supper finished with."

"No you aren't. You asked for work and there is work waiting for you. You can eat later," Justin said. Ethan got up with a smile on his face and started walking through the kitchen.

"Ethan no Justin he has to eat!" Molly yelled.

"No mama I'll eat later!" Ethan slowly said stopping just before opening the door.

"Molly he's waiting precious sun light." Molly didn't say anything after that and opened the door after Ethan walked out and yelled for the kids to come in and eat.

We had a quiet meal. Even the children didn't seem to want to talk. I hated that Ethan had to work through supper. He's going to have to stop sometime soon because it's getting dark. Well, the days are getting shorter. I really can't call it a day because I'm not sure which bed I'm going to sleep in? After about an hour has gone by I was waiting by the arch between the dining room and the kitchen waiting for Ethan to walk in. It's already 9 O'clock. The younger boys went to bed, and the girls are almost ready for bed. Molly's sitting in the family room talking to Elizabeth. Eric and Justin are just talking. I have this terrible feeling inside my stomach.

"Katherine he'll be in soon," Molly said.

"And how would you know?"

"Well he's worked outside late numerous of times before," she answered. I had to believe her. She's his mama. I couldn't stand any longer. As the girls left to go to sleep for the night, I sat down at the table facing the front door and waited for him there. Elizabeth and Eric then finally left for bed. Elizabeth rubbed my back and said good night. And Eric rubbed my back and said, "Glad that your home honey. Good night." And then he kissed my cheek.

Elizabeth is a lucky girl to have found Eric. Well at first, it was Eric finding Elizabeth. And at that time she wanted nothing to do with him, nothing. However, they are so cute with each other. I'm happy for the two.

After a while, Molly and Justin went to sleep. I then just laid my head down on the table to only rest my eyes.

After a while, I started to hear a noise from the kitchen. However, I was simply too tired to go see what it was. All of a sudden, I felt a hand against my back. I jerked up and started saying, "I've been lying I have money lots of it!" I tried to open my eyes, but it felt like they were nailed down shut.

"Katherine you're okay you were only dreaming."

"Ethan," I called out still trying to wake up. After a few seconds, I could see him, almost. He was sitting across from me eating.

"What time is it?" I asked. The room was dark but was filled with only little candle light.

"It's almost midnight," He said scooping up a spoon full of stew.

"Why were you sleeping down here instead of our bed?" And there he said it our bed. I wasn't sure if it was our bed or just his bed? I still haven't answered him yet.

"Oh I was just waiting for you," I said slowly still trying to wake up.

"Well I'm finish here. Let's get some rest," he said taking his bowl to the kitchen then coming back to the dining room. We both started walking up the stairs and into his room. We didn't even bother to change our clothes for what time it is. We only plopped down under the coverts and closed our beautiful eyes. I just realized that I told him the truth about myself. However, it's okay because he thought it was only a dream. Sleep falls upon us, and I start right back to dream.

Chapter 13

July 11, 1860 Evening

Dear Diary,

It's been a while scenes I've written. Lot's have happened. For example, the family coming over and a twister we had a few days ago. Starting with the family coming over it was Molly's side. There were a few cousins who were the same ages as Eric and Ethan. All of us older kids went down by the small river to go swimming. We swam and ate a little more. Then that evening all the family left to go home the following day. Well, some of them had to leave the next day. I believe the other half lives here in town.

The next day was scary for that, there was a twister. All of us had to run into the storm seller. Eric that day told the family that he had been courting Elizabeth. Justin and was alright with the news, and Molly was too scared to say anything because of the twister over our heads. However, when Ethan told them that he was courting me Molly didn't say anything like the first news, and Justin was ferries.

For some reason, and still to this day Justin, however, doesn't want us to be together. Everyday Justin and Ethan will get into fights. Molly, Eric, and I would have to stop them. There have been more fights breaking out now than I think this family has ever had before. July 7th Molly caught Ethan, and I was only sleeping in his bed, and she got angry with us. It was more with him. You see she was trying to find me, and madness happened. Now to think about it, I never did go and see what she wanted me for?

That evening Justin was naming terrible things about Ethan and me. Then Ethan punched Justin in the noise! Justin got what he disserved. Then Ethan and I left and stayed two nights at the Greenfield Inn just to get away from the family.

The next day we had lunch out in the woods, and Ethan was playing with me saying there was a bear. He moved away from the tree we were sitting by and jumped at me to knock us both down. Oh was I scared. He did that because I asked him a question about his family. I started walking back to town, and he yelled from the distant that I was going the wrong way. Then I admitted to him that I got embarrassed by him. He finally said sorry and that he was only trying to make memories.

Then the next day we made it home and Ethan had to work outside the rest of the night. I stayed well tried to stay up and waited for him. He doesn't know that I admitted to him after he tried to wake me up about the lie Elizabeth, and I have and about the money. He thought it was only a dream I had, and yet he still didn't question it. I must go.

Earlier Ethan and Eric were teaching Elizabeth and me how to drive the wagon. We had some difficulties. However, the four of us had a fun time, and we trusted each other. Then the boys showed us how to ride a horse. Our butts started hurting when we were finished! We all had a great time, and we'll be learning later. I love to write in you my diary, and I may stop writing in you for a while, I'm not sure?

Love Katherine

...

Down stairs is the same by which Molly is cooking dinner and the children either helping or playing outside. I look out the window in the kitchen to see Elizabeth and Eric sitting on the front porch steps. Elizabeth has her head lying on his shoulder. Molly looks over towards me as she was moving some strands of hair out of her eyes.

"Oh good your down stairs," she started to say. That sounded like what my mama would say to me.

"Is there anything you want me to do for you?" I asked her.

"Yes I have a few things I need you to take up to the children's room." She handed me a blanket, and some dolls that the girls had left. She said that they must go in Emma and Marty's room. They were both outside playing with Samuel and Jeffery.

Once in their room, I sat down on I believed to be Marty's bed. I also believe that she is sharing this bed with Emma ever scenes Elizabeth, and I moved in. Marty had a book lying wide open to the middle of the book on her bed. It looked to be a diary. Marty has a diary? That's just different to see. I leaned over to try to skim over what she wrote. I didn't start reading it because it was her privet thoughts. All of a sudden, there were footsteps coming up the stairs. I assumed it was either Eric or Elizabeth or one of the boys. Then Marty started to walk in and afterwards stopped in the middle of the doorway.

"What are you doing?" she asked.

"Marty I was told to bring up this blanket and your dolls," I tried to smile. She was still standing in the doorway.

"No you were about to read my diary weren't you?" she raised her voice.

"No Marty I would never do that to you," I explained.

"Yes you were; you were about to read my diary!" she cried as she stomped her left foot on the ground hard. Then she ran away. I stood up quick yelling, "Marty wait. Marty let's talk about this!" I ran after her.

Once down stairs we ran passed Molly which even she couldn't get her saying out on time as I was chasing her daughter. Marty ran through the open door as did I. I had to run through Eric and Elizabeth, which slowed me down. She was fast for her age. I finally caught up with her out by the back fence. She had her hand holding onto the middle rail as she was staring at the ground. I slowly started walking up to her.

"Marty," I called out calmly.

"Go away. I don't want you!" she cried at me. I wasn't going to be the weaker one here. She possibly thinks she is the bigger person.

"Marty I'm not going until you hear me out," I stopped and waited to see if she was going to say anything else.

"Marty I need you to believe me that I didn't read your diary. I was only admiring it. I know what it's like to not have your privacy," I said hoping that she got what I said. I stepped a little closer towards her. I still got nothing out of her.

"I need for you to believe me!" I cried out. She turned her head just a bit to see me.

"And I don't want to believe you! You came here and ruined things!"

"Ruined what?" She then stood up while whipping a few tears away.

"You ruined my family, every day, there's yelling going on, and it was never like that!" and then she ran away from me to a different place to cry. Just as she stared to run I called out, "Marty?" However, I was too late.

I slowly started walking to the house. Marty's just a hard child to get through. She never wants to listen well. When I reached the front porch, Eric and Elizabeth weren't there sitting this time. I opened the door to look inside. Molly was still cooking. She turned around and came close to me.

"What's going on with Marty?" she asked. I know I shouldn't tell her about Marty having a diary, I mean its Marty's secret.

"Don't worry Molly, I dealt with it," I whispered. Molly gave me a grin and turned around to finish cooking. Molly had me, and Madison set the table up this evening. While setting up the table I thought to myself a few days ago, the family had stopped saying a prayer before their meal. Maybe we're all prayed out or something like that? Molly comes in with the basket of rolls and the pitcher of water.

It was time to eat now. Molly went back to the kitchen to open the front door to yell out supper's ready. Everyone started to come in one at a time. Eric and Elizabeth slowly came down the stairs. I saw Marty coming in through the door right after her father did. Molly brought the pot of stew from the kitchen. We then all started to sit.

I was sitting at the end of the table tonight. I had a better lookout to see everyone. I kept a good eye on Marty. Not so much where she felt uncomfortable. I slowly ate feeling embarrassed again. I didn't mean to make Marty feel like that tonight.

Marty was right about how we came and ruined things. I feel really bad about it thinking that it's my fault. Once again, we had another quiet evening. Lately Ethan has been having one of the girls or boys to sit next to Justin all because he just doesn't want to be next to him. He'll only work with him, and that's it. After everyone was finished eating the girls helped Molly clean up. I left to go outside and swing. After a while, the door opens up and Marty slowly walks out with what looks to be her diary coming my way.

"Marty," I said slowly acting all surprised to see her.

"Here take it. I don't want it any more. Go ahead and read my life. The first page will say everything!" she yelled throwing me her diary, which then fell to the ground. Marty ran away after that crying outback. I picked up the book and opened to the first page. I started reading.

Dear Diary May 1859

I wish I knew how to read and write.

That was all on the first page. I flipped through all the other pages, and they were the equivalent lengths. Small simple and all said the same thing but with different spelling. Some of the pages had some unusual things in them like when Justin hit Molly and her. I would read more, but the spelling is making it hard for me to read why? I feel like Marty was only trying to blame Elizabeth and myself for all the yelling when it's been going on this whole time. I stopped myself before I could go any further. I didn't want to go any further.

I had an idea that I hope Marty will like and let me do and for the other girls and boys. I started walking into the house. As I was walking up to my room, I was thinking that I could help the children to read and write! Oh this will finally give me an opportunity to help out more and to feel a part of the family and to get my mind off of my lie. You know in order to help them; I need lots of paper and books. I only have so little paper left. I'm determent to do this. I clenched my fist and grabbed my writing utensil and wrote on that first page in Marty's diary saying.

Dear Marty's diary,

July 11, 1860 Late Evening

Dear Marty, there is hope in everything. You just have to believe in yourself and find it. I am here for you if you truly want my help. I do care for you and love you. You are a special girl.

Love Katherine

I was sitting on her bed when writing this down. Sooner or later, I started to hear footsteps again, and then it was Marty walking in. She was just standing there staring at me with her eyes red and puffy from crying.

"Marty," I started to say calmly. She held out her hand at a stopping point and said, "No!" I wasn't going to give in, not now. I stood up still holding her book.

"Marty will you just listen to me?"

"No Katherine. Look I know you already read my diary, and now you know my secret. So go and tell it to everyone. I dare you too," she breathed hard. I had no choice but to sit her down and make her listen to me. I came towards her quick and grabbed her arms and forced her to sit to hear me out. She was screaming at the time, "No, no, no I won't Katherine! Just leave me alone!"

"Marty listen to what I have to say to you. Your secret is safe with me. I won't tell. I want you to understand. I want you to understand me!" I yelled. She started to kick her legs and scream even louder. I was hoping at this time Molly and the others weren't hearing this. After grabbing her and just closing the door, there was a loud knock and yelling going on outside.

"Girls what's going on in there?" Molly yelled.

"Molly I have it," I yelled.

"Marty please listen. Just calm down," I tried my best for her to hear me. We finally got to sit on the bed.

"No Katherine, no," still yelling.

"No," still yelling.

"No." She was now crying at this point.

"No," still crying. Then she finally buried her head into my lap. I glided my hand over her head calming her down. I believed Molly went down stairs and hopes to not have a care of what just happened.

Marty sat up and stared at me with two swollen red eyes.

"Marty would you like for me to teach you how to read and write?" I asked calmly and slowly. She stared at me whipping the tears away then I helped her to hope she knew that I cared.

"Yes please," she whispered and came in quick and hugged me.

"We'll start tomorrow," I said to her with a half smile. I got up and left her in her room so she could wash up for bed and so no one will notice that she's been crying.

"Katherine," she asked for me before I was just about to leave to go down stairs.

"Yes," I stared back standing in the middle of the door frame.

"Thank you for getting through to me, I mean…"

"Marty your welcome," I interrupted her.

"Thank you," she murmured. My heart went to this warm feeling all over. I only smiled back at her as she was sitting on her bed with her hands folded in her lap.

Chapter 14

July
July 15th Marty and Emma just turned fourteen. July 22 was the same as always. July 30 is the same as usual.

August

September

October we start new. October 8th is a different story. The past few months us children were told that we were having company over. It was one of Justin's longtime old friend and his daughter. I've been told that Molly, and the rest of the younger children don't like Justin's friend and his daughter. Eric and Ethan have grown to not liking them either.

October 10th is a new story of the day we start. I'm outside on the front porch swing writing in my diary.

October 10, 1860 Noon

Dear Diary,

In the last few months, I have been slowly teaching Marty to read and write. After the first month, the other girls found out and also want to learn how to read and write. It all was taking too much of my time and paper. I had to tell Elizabeth about this in order to have reinforcements. Then after a while I had to let Molly know all about this. Right now, we are already at the beginning of October. I don't exactly remember what day that was but the next-day Molly and Eric, and I left to go to town to buy a full package of paper, writing utensils and books. And they came in handy.

Eric, Ethan, and Justin still don't know anything about this. Then a few days later the younger boys found out and also want to learn how to read and write. So Elizabeth and I had even more to work with.

There's something about Marty that I don't just understand about? I'll be teaching them everything being identical at the same time slowly so they will understand how it sounds, looks, and how to write it. However, she would either make it look an unusual way and then sound something different than what it honestly should sound. I'm not sure if she is just playing with me, or she really doesn't get these things? I worry for her.

I need to go; a wagon just pulled into the drive. I believe it must be the friend of Justin. They said what their names were months ago, but I can't remember them at all.

Love Katherine

...

I sat there narrowing my eyes on the older man and his daughter who looked to be mine and Elizabeth age. Still in the wagon I knew she kept her eyes on me. I was sitting there waiting for someone to come up to the wagon. Justin, Ethan, and Eric came out from the barn. Justin was hooting and hollering. Molly and the younger children came out to see what was going on. Elizabeth stayed back behind with me. We all gathered around the wagon.

Justin came close to the wagon and gave his friend a hand down while saying, "How was the trip John?"

"Oh it was fine. We made it on time last night here in town," he said. His daughter was just sitting in the wagon up front fluffing out her purple dress. I could tell that they were rich in the looks of their clothes. They had quite a lot luggage with them. However, I'm surprised that they didn't ride stagecoach.

"How are you Malinda," Justin asked politely. She just smiled at him. Then she stood up and swung both arms out saying, "Oh Ethan; Ethan is that you?" I gazed over towards Ethan's way as he had a grin on his face.

"Oh my goodness have you grown boy. You're a man now!" she screeched. "Well you aren't just going to leave me up, here are you? Now be a gentleman and help me down will you?" she demanded. Ethan moved to get up to her and helped her down slowly. All she did was had her arms on his shoulders, and she only had to jump down. I did hate that she practically grabbed his hands and forced them on her waist. Once down she gave Elizabeth and me a good long stare. She was scanning our faces.

This girl here looks spoiled and probably damans everything that she wants. She was pale to the color with long blond hair and with blue eyes. She almost looked like Elizabeth.

The past few months we've been discussing generally about the bedroom sleeping arrangements again. We weren't sure, on how long they were staying. Only that it was said for maybe two months, but that would put them to leave around December, and that's too cold for anyone to leave to go home. I believe that they'll have to stay even longer.

"Shall we head inside for some coffee?" Molly asked all of us. Half of us nodded our heads and smiled. Justin and his friend led the way into the house as the rest trailed behind. The men, including Ethan and Eric went and sat down in the dining room to talk. Molly and Elizabeth worked together to prepare the coffee. Malinda and I stood there watching them. Just from watching out of the corner of my eye, I could tell that she was watching me.

"Hello My names Malinda Miller," she said finally facing me. I turned and smiled saying, "Hello my names Katherine Stone and this is Elizabeth Kent." Elizabeth smiled while whipping her hands with her apron.

"So are you a friend of Ethan?" she asked. I was thinking about what to say to her.

"Um yes, I am a friend of Ethan a really good friend!" I murmured quietly after a really good friend. She smiles then looks on past me; I believe that is what she was doing. All of a sudden, the men started walking past us and were heading outside.

"Father where you men going," Malinda laughed.

"Oh Malinda we're only going out to the barn," her father answered. Eric came up to Elizabeth to whisper something in her ear. Malinda was watching them as I saw her eye brows narrow down. Ethan was long gone with Justin, and Eric had to run to catch up with them.

They were maybe going out to the barn not to hear us women, or so that we could sit down and talk. Molly had the coffee ready, and we all moved in the dining room to drink. Elizabeth sat next to me as Malinda sat across from us. Molly was at the end of the table pouring the hot coffee into our cups.

"Malinda how's your mother doing," Molly asked.

"She's doing fine. She and father got divorced almost a little over a year ago." Molly was sipping her coffee and as Malinda said divorced she nearly chocked.

"I'm so sorry to hear that child."

"Mother and father for years never got along. She moved back in with her parent's plantation," she said sipping her coffee.

I remember someone saying to me that this family is from Georgia a southern state with slaves. It's hotter down there than it is right here. However, now since its October, it has been getting cooler. We should be harvesting the fields by now?

"So Katherine is that right?" Malinda asked me. I just said my name to her less than three minute ago.

"That's right," I say only smiling.

"I was here just two years ago, and I never knew you. When and how did you two became friends?"

"Well Elizabeth and I were just new to this town, and we didn't know where anything was. Elizabeth left me to go somewhere, and I didn't hear what she said to me. I started walking out in the middle of the road and started to hear everyone yelling," I started to explain. I was staring into her eyes watching every movement. Left then right then back to left again. She was studding me.

"There was a man in a wagon charging at me. I tripped and fell. Next I knew I was being grabbed by my arm and then fell on someone. It was Ethan who saved me," I finished. "They never did catch the man in the wagon. And I've been back in town a few times and never did ask the sheriff about that day," I added. I have never really processed that day in my head. I only looked at it as a day not a day that I met my love!

"My man is growing up so much!" she cheered.

"Eric and I have been courting for a few months," Elizabeth said out in the open. Molly smiled at her.

"So how far away do you two live," she asked. I can really hear the southern tone Malinda gives off when she speaks. I looked over at Elizabeth.

"Well just up stairs in a separate bedroom from the boys," Elizabeth said. Malinda was almost about to take another drink of her coffee then stopped as Elizabeth said upstairs.

"Oh really now," she asked lifting one eyebrow.

"Malinda we were going to talk to you and your father about how the sleeping arrangements were going to be," Molly added on for a slight change of mood, maybe? Malinda shifts her head over towards Molly and continues sipping her coffee. The whole time I watched her, while keeping my mug up just hovering over my lips. I could feel the mug burning my lips. Then I pulled it back away so that I don't burn them.

"Yes Molly!" she smiled bright.

"We were going to move Jeffery and Samuel over with Eric and Ethan. Savanna and Madison were once moved in with Marty and Emma. However, we were going to move them back into their room. We thought that Marty and Emma needed their room again," Molly laughed just a bit trying to make it seem funny. Elizabeth gave off a little noise too.

Finally after two hours, the men came in and sat down for supper. We were all in different sets than we are used to. This time I wasn't sitting next to Ethan but Malinda was too on the other side. This made me feel weird.

Chapter 15

October 11th

October 12th

October 13th

October 14th

October 15th all of our days were the same.

October 16th. Just two hours before lights out Ethan and I have not once had any alone time together. I finally got to have him, while he is still eighteen.

"Are you excited about tomorrow?" I asked him. We were cuddling up under his blankets holding each other.

"What's tomorrow?" he asks smiling like he has no clue.

"You do to know what's tomorrow. You and Eric should know," I laughed. He leans in closer towards me. I love to count how many freckles he has under his eyes and on his nose.

"I'm not sure if I'm excited about tomorrow. I just want tonight to never end," he whispered then kissing me. I don't want tonight to ever end. We stop kissing, and Ethan lifts up his head. I slowly started to open my eyes.

"I hope Eric remembers what's tomorrow?" he teased. I laughed hard then started to cough.

"Whoa now whoa," he would say.

We were still in our day clothes. I had on my blue blouse with my yellow skirt. Ethan had his same-old dirty brown pair of trousers with a stained up button shirt. He has other clothes it's just he really does not like to change. Eric, on the other hand, will strip down anywhere. Just the other day Molly was yelling at him for taking off his shirt in the middle of the family room when our guesses are here.

All of a sudden, the door slams open and Ethan, and I sat up quick. We must have fallen asleep for a while. It must have been no longer than twenty-five minutes or so. Malinda said something right when she opened the door, but I couldn't hear what she said because Ethan and I also made a noise when we woke up.

"Oh my goodness I'm sorry. I hope I didn't disturb anything between you two," she said standing in the middle of the doorway. I immediately got out of Ethan's bed and stood there. Ethan stood up next to me.

"Malinda can I help you with anything," he asked clearing his throat.

"No Ethan I'm fine," she said with her southern accent.

"I think I'll go to bed," I said and started to walk out. However, Malinda didn't want to move out of my way.

I looked back over towards Ethan, who just stood there.

"Excuse me," I said under my breath staring at the floor.

"Now hold on just a minute I want to know what's going on between you two!" she laughed. I stood back to where Ethan was standing. He moved his arm to my lower back.

"Malinda, I have been courting Katherine since July."

"Wow and you never thought about seeding me a letter with the news. Ethan you're my friend." I could say otherwise about her and Ethan. Whenever she talks, it's always with a laugh and or a smirk. In the last few days, Malinda has been a pain in my butt about Ethan. He is mine, not yours.

"Malinda, I think you need to go. We'll talk about it later," Ethan said, and then he led the way out of his room and into mine.

"Ethan," I started to say while walking into the dark unlit room. I was standing in the middle of my room watching him close the door and just standing there in front of it. He turned around and stared at me saying, "What?"

"Ethan I'm fine, just go to bed." You could hear hooting and hollering and laughing going on down stairs.

"Okay Katherine," he had said coming in close kissing me next moving his hair out of his eyes. He turned around and left the room. He left the door half open for the light to shine through just barely.

I scrambled around on the desk to find a match. Elizabeth had out all her things everywhere in the room. It was a mess because of her. I finally found one and lit all the candles. It brought a warm glow to the room. I sat down on my bed just staring at the floor thinking. Ethan and Malinda were talking in his bedroom. I couldn't hear much just a mumble here and there.

My door opens up slowly, and Elizabeth comes walking in and sits down next to me.

"You okay," she asks moving her arm around my shoulder. I stare into her eyes.

"No I'm not. I feel embarrassed sort of," I say to her in a whisper. Just before she could say anything, I interrupt her.

"Ethan and I accidentally fell asleep in his room just now, and Malinda walked in on us. We were just sleeping and only sleeping nothing else. It was by accident. She was to never know about Ethan and I. That's what Ethan had said to me the other night," I whispered under my breath. She didn't say anything after that. Until she whispered, "Your fine Katherine," then she gave me a kiss on my check.

"How about we get some sleep," she said standing up throwing me my nightgown that I had laid on the trunk. We changed out of our clothes then covered up for the night. Sleep was the last thing I had in mind. We only had one blanket for the both of us. It's the middle of October and its cold. The family is poor in the winter months as I was told. It's hard for them to stay warm.

So Elizabeth and I gave the rest of our blankets to Savanna and Madison. Elizabeth and I are big enough to use each other's body heat for warmth. When I sleep with Ethan some nights, he'll fall asleep quicker than me, and he can really give off a lot of body heat. Elizabeth can hardly, but I'm sure Eric does the same like his brother. The room was half lit by this point. One of the candles went out. Once the girls and everybody else went to sleep it was dark upstairs. The girls prefer the door to be left open just a tad. They only like it that way.

I lay there in bed staring up at the ceiling thinking. It could be midnight or one o'clock by now, and I am still not asleep. It's not from my little rest I had early with Ethan. No I'm just thinking too much about different things. I wasn't expecting things to end like this. For starters running away from home, then falling in love, and now Malinda, who I hate who thinks she's better than me.

Just in one of the other rooms I hear some mumbling, rumbling, thumps, footsteps? Whatever you would call it; I heard it. I lay there still in bed. Elizabeth wanted to sleep on the outside, and I wasn't going to argue with her about it. So I was put against the wall. It makes it harder for me to get up if I get up before her. However, I manage to try.

The noise was footsteps sliding on the wooden floor. It stopped by my door. I thought to myself why bother to even look? My first thought of who it was would be Ethan. Maybe checking up on me or just sleep walking.

"Katherine," a really soft faint voice calls out. Ethan defiantly pops right into my mind. I sat up slowly hoping not to disturb Elizabeth. Trying to get out of bed was the thing. However, I still manage to get out. I walked over to the door with my arms held out.

"Ethan," I called out under my breath.

"By the door," he would say. How dumb do you think I am? I open the door a tad bit more. It was still half way open for the girls, but I had to move it to see him better. I can see his face, his round shaped face. He reached out his arms by my waist. I was shivering at this point, and he knew it. My head laid gently on his chest as one of his hands came holding my head down harder. I knew that he didn't want to let go.

"I'm sorry for what happened back there. Will you forgive me?"

"Yes," I said lifting my head up and taking a step backward.

"Why are you still up," I asked.

"I couldn't sleep and I was thinking of you way too much."

I said nothing after that and just stroke my hand on the side of his face down to his cheek. He tilted his head, just as I was doing this. He leaned in close and started to kiss me. It was another long kiss. It was really a good night; I truly love you kiss.

We stopped and I said, "Happy 19th birthday Ethan!" He chuckled but not loud.

"Yes I forgot," he said slowly and sad. I walked away as so did he. I fidget my way back into bed trying not to wake up Elizabeth. Once in bed I turned to my side facing the wall and closed my eyes and drifted off dreaming.

Chapter 16

Elizabeth has been up for about an hour longer than me. I lay on my bed reading this bible I have that Molly gave to me a few months back. I'm reading it to try to understand how things work here. My family isn't religious, and I've said this many of the times. I look over to my right to see that Madison and Savanna are still sleeping. I decide to get up and go down stairs. I've already had been dressed for the day. I only want to lay in bed to relax.

I walk down stairs with a smile on my face then to find Malinda and Ethan sitting next to each other at the table. Eric and Elizabeth were sitting next to them. I basically wasted a perfectly good smile on this day. I stood there like I just saw a ghost. I shook my head and said, "Good morning!"

"Good morning Katherine," Eric says standing up and putting his hand on my shoulder. Molly comes walking in from outside.

"Girls can you go and collect eggs and feed for me," Molly asked and next added, "And I'll go milk the cow." I stare at Elizabeth and turn my head towards Molly and said, "Yes ma'am." Elizabeth and I started to walk out. As I opened the door Elizabeth grabbed the basket for eggs then hand it to me. Elizabeth and I were just half way to the hen house before we started to hear someone calling to us.

"Oh wait, wait for me!" Malinda called out waving her arm. We stopped and waited for her to catch up. We were only a few feet away from the hen house.

"You know I'd like to help you," she said smiling away.

"Oh Malinda you can help us," Elizabeth said trying to make her feel a part of our friendship. Elizabeth opens the door to let us in. Malinda went in before me holding up part of her dress. Then it was me and lastly Elizabeth. The hens were all still in their beds sleeping this morning. We all sort of gotten up earlier than usual so that's why. I would grab the eggs or egg depending on how many they would lay and put them in the basket. Elizabeth would grab the pale of feed and throw it on the ground. Malinda was just standing there watching us still holding her dress up.

"Malinda, are you going to help us," Elizabeth asked.

"No, I don't want to get my dress all dirty," she laughed. No she wasn't getting her dress all dirty, but her shoes were another thing. Malinda was wearing a dark purple dress from head to toe. Just around her waist line was a yellow lace ribbon sown on. Malinda is well maybe a little richer than Elizabeth, and I was. And I say this when we did have money. When we first started to live here we had to put away the thought about our old lives behind. No more fancy parties, dresses, and rides.

What Elizabeth has on is just her yellow blouse and her blue skirt. I have my pink blouse with my brown skirt on. It's my favorite dress to wear. To be honest we like this life better. We have a small house that is filled with love, hate, hope, shame, friendship, and most of all family. They are poor but still strong to move through it.

"Well I believe we're done here," I said standing up after putting the last egg in the basket. Malinda waited by the door until I came and pull it open for us. When we got back to the house, Molly started cooking breakfast. I tried to look for the boys, but they might have gone to the barn.

"Are the children up yet," I asked. Elizabeth didn't hesitate to start helping Molly. She also hasn't answered me yet. Malinda and I were standing there in the kitchen watching them while we're doing nothing. I thought to myself that I could just go ahead and see. I left the kitchen and started walking up the stairs. As I was walking up stairs, Emma and Marty passed me smiling. Once up stairs, I see Eric walking out of his room with the boys following behind him. He gazed over at me with a smile.

In my room, the girls were already up and getting dressed.

"Katherine will you do my hair for me," Savanna asked sitting at the desk waiting for me. I didn't answer instead I just started to brush her hair for her. Madison was talking as I was listening while I was braiding Savanna's hair back. As I finished Savanna got up and Madison sat down for her hair to be braided. Then after her, I sat down to brush my hair and started to braid it back. We were talking for a while about how to do other hair styles.

"Breakfast," a voice called out from down stairs. We were talking the whole time, so I think it was Elizabeth that said it. We started to head down stairs and take our seats.

I was just about to take a seat next to Ethan until Malinda sat next to him. He was at the far end corner with Justin setting at the end and John setting across from Ethan. Setting next to Malinda was Marty and Emma. Then it was Madison and Savanna. Molly was at the other end across from Justin. I was sitting next to Molly across from Savanna. Eric was sitting on my left side of me with Elizabeth on his left. On the right of John were Sam and Jeff. This was how we were. It took nearly five minutes to figure out where we were all going to sit at. And it's weird because other days aren't like this.

"I believe we should pray before we start to eat," Molly said out loud, so we all could hear. We bowed our heads and held each other's hands and said a prayer in our heads. I honestly didn't know what to say so I said this, "Dear Lord thank you for this morning meal we are about to eat." I suck at saying prayers. After that we raised our heads and started passing the food around. Ethan started with the pancakes, and I started with the eggs, and the biscuits were somewhere?

I believe Molly is going to be doing a lot of cooking today. During the whole time, we all were eating. I was staring at Ethan. Justin, John, and Malinda were talking about themselves. The girls would talk with each other, and Molly was talking with Elizabeth and Eric. Ethan was only eating, listening, and also watching me. We would smile back in forth. Talk with our eyes and with how we would move our hair out of our face.

After a while, Malinda caught on with what we were doing. After that she started to talk to Ethan and only Ethan and both fathers. They would be talking about what kind of man she was going to marry and then give an example saying it would be Ethan.

"I want a tall, strong, hard worker. Just like you Ethan," she would say loud enough for me to hear.

"I want two children and a big house with servants." Her, her father and Justin would not stop talking about Malinda's future. She would have her eyes on him. He would have his eyes either on mine or hers.

I could feel my heart pounding harder. Suddenly, I felt a hand grabbing mine. It was Eric's hand holding mine under the table. I would look him in the eyes, and I could see in his that he saw what I was seeing over there. He knew what I was feeling inside. Alternatively, maybe he thought I was about to climb over the table and slap Malinda until she starts to cry. That was only a thought I also had in mind.

Eric would then finally let go to help his mother with the dishes. Elizabeth and I would also help. We all went our separate ways after eating. All we had to do was to wash the dishes. I knew Justin and John went out on the porch to talk. And the children were in the family room playing with their dolls and solders. But I didn't know where Malinda and Ethan were? I wasn't going to go and hunt them down. I really had nothing else to do but to go and write in my diary. So I started walking to my room. Upstairs I heard some voices in Ethan's room. As I walked up slowly, I could see that his door was open. It was funny because it was wide open. So I walked up as normal but then had to stop just before passing his room.

I knew before they were talking, but I couldn't make out of what because it was more like whispers. The talking stopped, but I didn't hear any whispering. I walked in front of the door and stopped. I stood there watching him kissing her on Eric's bed. I wasn't sure on if I made a noise, but I did put my hand over my mouth. I knew my eyes got big, and my heart started to pound faster. I started to run down stairs crying.

"Katherine," Ethan called my name. I heard him running out of his room and down the stairs after me.

"Katherine wait!" he yelled, but I didn't. Just as I was about to open the door he comes up behind me and slams it shut. I was breathing hard, and I could hear him doing the same. Molly was in the kitchen watching as was Elizabeth.

"Wait, it's not what it looks like," he whispered, but I didn't want to listen to him, so I elbowed him in the gut. He fell onto the floor as I slammed the door open and ran. I could hear Molly saying to Elizabeth,

"Let her be." I ran out to the field that was in front of the house with Ethan following slowly behind. I stopped as soon as I knew if I was far enough. I then fell to my knees. Ethan was still yelling my name, "Katherine!" I stood up as he came closer to me. The only thing that I thought was best was to push him, so I did. He just stands there saying my name repeatedly.

"It's not what it looks like?" I would say to him angrily.

"Katherine, she kissed me. She came up and started touching me, and she forced me to kiss her!" I tried to push him again, but he stopped me. He grabbed my arm and was holding it tight. I let out a faint scream because he was hurting me.

"Ethan you're hurting me," I cried.

"Katherine it wasn't me. She came at me and started kissing me," he cried. I then fell to the ground from the pain he was giving me. I was thinking to myself why, why are you doing this to me? And then he finally let go of my arm.

"I love you, Katherine," he cried. My mind was in a thousand places. I sit there watching him whip his tears down.

"And I don't love you," I whispered. I mean I couldn't believe I said that. He stares me down.

"What did you say, you don't love me?" he said angry narrowing his big puffy brown eyes. He would start to walk back and forth swaying his arms around.

"I want you to stand up and say it to my face," He yelled. Then he forced me to stand up. He grabbed a hold of both my arms. I stood up aggressively. We were personally close at this point. We were so close I could feel him breathing on me. His warm breathe felt good on my cold nose.

"I don't love you and I never will," I said angrily. We both narrowed our eyes at each other.

"And I never will love you ever again Katherine." He turns around and starts to head back to the house. I called out his name, "Ethan wait, wait!" I then ran to him and hit him on the shoulder. He turned around angrily.

"I hate you; I hate you, and I hate you!" I screamed while still hitting him.

"And I never want to see you. I never want to talk to you ever again, you here," he would scream at the same time as I was. We then started pointing fingers. I would slap him on the face. He would only push me back gently.

"I wish I would have never saved you that first day we met!"

"And I wish I never had to leave my home and meet you and lie to your family!" and there I yelled out the truth. Now the only thing I need to worry about is that if he notices what I said was true. And it hurts inside that he wished he had never saved me.

"You lied to me and my family after we gave you a place to live?" he asked whipping some spit away from his mouth. I ran my fingers through my hair of what came out of my braid.

"Yes Ethan I lied to you and your family. I lied saying that my family kicked me out of my house. However, what honestly happened was that I was going to be forced to marry a man whom I truthfully didn't know." I stopped in order to breathe. I was done talking to him.

"Who the hell are you? Are you lying to me about your name too?"

"No Ethan and what about you lying to me about not kissing Malinda? I saw you." We dissent apart after bickering. He came walking fast towards me. I took a few steps back because it looked like he was coming to attack me.

"What are you doing Ethan?" I screamed. We were now closer than we were before.

"No I was not lying to you. And you will never say anything like that ever again," he yelled raising a hand up to make it look like he was going to hit me. We started to slow down our breathing. I would shiver and still cry. Ethan then turned around and started walking back to the house once again. I cried out nonsense and fell back to the ground and looked away from the house.

"Oh my Lord, Ethan," I whispered under my breath. It's still morning not even 10 o'clock, and we already had a fight. I can't believe we're over, through, done for it. This day sucks, and it's all because of her. The crying hurts, and it's not the only thing that hurts. The breathing is hard, and my hands are wet from the tears. I hate him. I hate me.

I didn't know what to do or what to say to the family. I've been sitting here on the ground crying for nearly fifteen minutes or so. I decide that I should get up and go in the house and up to my room. I stumbled while getting up and walking to the house. I saw that Justin, John, and Eric were on the porch smoking sugars that John brought with him. Eric was out with them and wasn't smoking. As I was walking Eric stepped off the porch and was walking towards me. I knew he was walking toward me, but I wasn't going to stop for him.

"Katherine, wait," he said.

"Eric I really don't feel like talking," I said with a weak voice shoving him out of the way. We were only a few steps away from the porch. He then pulled out his arm to stop me. I slowly closed in on him and fell into him crying.

"Eric please," I cried softly.

"It's okay. You'll be fine," he would say quieting me down. Next to Ethan, Eric has been there for me as a friend. Ethan makes me smile and makes me feel good about myself when I can't or so he did. Eric makes me laugh. Elizabeth is a lucky girl to have Eric for her love.

We looked up at each other, and he whispered, "Let's go up stairs and Elizabeth will come too." He held me around the arm. Eric led the way in the house as Elizabeth without asking any questions followed behind us. I was keeping a look out for Ethan and Malinda. I saw that they both were sitting in the family room watching us go up stairs. I gazed over to see his eyes. They were narrow and cold.

Once in my room, I sat down on the bed and just stared at the floor. Elizabeth was begging me into telling her what happened between us. So I looked up and stared her in the eyes. I told her the truth. After that she started to raise her voice and Eric had to shut her up. I know he was surprised too, but yet he understood. The three of us stayed up here until dinner was ready. Elizabeth and Eric stood up and started walking to the door until they looked back at me.

"Aren't you coming," Elizabeth asked.

"No I can't I'm not hungry," I said. They stare and leave. I wasn't hungry. I hope Molly will understand, and I hope she won't get mad at me too. You miss one meal you have to skip the next one until whichever one is coming up.

I just lay in bed crying and hurting. I would take what happened and go through it a few times in my head. Then I would go through it in different ways in my head. Why did they have to come? Why did she have to be here? Why did he have to kiss her? Why? And yet I still lie here whimpering. I would try to close my eyes but all I would see is his face. I'm discussed by it.

Later on, footsteps were coming up and then would stop just outside my door. I would have to stop crying just so no one could hear. Then my door opens up, and Molly comes in and sits on the foot of my bed. She's just sitting there watching the floor. I then sat up thinking that she wouldn't say anything until I sat up but still nothing. She won't even look at me.

"Eric and Elizabeth told me what happened," she had finally said.

"I knew they would have or Ethan," my voice cracked. "Molly I'm sorry for lying to you and your family, but we needed a place to live. We only had so much money. We never spent it. Do you want it? I can give it to you in exchange, and we can leave right now," I said quickly.

"Katherine stop!" she finally looked up at me.

"Katherine I don't want your money, and I don't want you two to leave either, your family now. The truth would have been better at the beginning, but I understand." Yeah I understand too when I asked her about her past husbands. Molly then stood up and turned my way saying, "I'm only giving you today to stay up here and not come down to eat. The pain will go away trust me," and then she left me.

Part of me believes her that the pain will go away, but the other part of me says no it won't. I lie back down to rest and cry. If I fall asleep, then I know I will start to dream. My dream would consist, him and me or at least something about him. And now I sleep.

I wake up to see Elizabeth at the foot of our bed. She had a plate filled with food and a smile on her face.

"Morning," she said.

"Is it morning did I sleep that long?" I asked sitting up quickly. She started to laugh a little and said, "No it's not morning I was only saying that. We all just got done with supper, and Molly made you a plate since the last time you ate was breakfast." She hands over the plate to me as I start to wolf it down. There were mashed potatoes with gravy and deer meat that was roasted. Then after I was finished Elizabeth pulled out from behind her two plates with a slice of cake on them.

"Molly and I backed a cake. And you know this was my first time too," she said.

"I'm proud of you," I tried to smile.

"You know this was for their birthday?" she said after handing me the plate.

"Yes I know," I said afterwards. I took a long look at the cake. It tasted to be vanilla. We were eating it in silence.

"You know you could think of this cake just for Eric," she said smiling. I smiled back at her saying, "Your right."

After we got done eating Elizabeth took the plates down stairs and then everyone was coming up stairs to get ready for bed. I got dressed as did the girls. Malinda and her father would be talking in their room. Elizabeth and Eric were out in the hallway whispering and sort of kissing maybe? Then she finally came in. I was watching her, and I saw that Eric was following her. He kissed Savanna and Madison good night then came to kiss my forehead.

Then he slowly moved his fingers to move some hair strands aside from my ear. "I'm sorry and I love you," he whispered to me, and he walked out the bedroom. He gave Elizabeth a long gaze before leaving. She truly is lucky to have him. I lie down and roll over to close my eyes.

I think one last time about him and only say in my head; *Love doesn't come through time.*

Chapter 17

November 7, 1860 Early Morning,

Dear Diary,

Twenty-one days have already gone by since I've talked to Ethan. Wow it's funny to see his name written out. Molly was right that the pain will go away. However, instead, I feel numb or frustrated. When I look at him, I see nothing or a blur. I try my best not to stare at him, but it's a force of habit. Living under the same roof is hard. Elizabeth and I are thankful for Molly letting us still live here.

Today Elizabeth just turned eighteen. She is really feeling down. She always spends this day with her parents because it's the one day she asks from them to spend it as a family. I write this because I am thankful for my mama and father to take an hour out of their day and spend it with me in our studies.

I miss how father would read the paper out loud and how mama would be crocheting a scarf or a small towel. I miss the little things that I didn't see much out of them the most. Elizabeth doesn't have that with her parents. Her father just likes to work, and her mother only drinks tea and talks to her friends when they come over. Mine and Elizabeth's father have worked together for some time it seems. And yet mine will still have some time with me. Ever since they both moved up here years ago from George, they have worked together.

I really do miss my family, but what I don't miss was the man I was to marry. Who knows what I would be doing at this moment with him? Well, I need to leave to help out down stairs. I'm missing a part of my heart.

Love Katherine

. . .

I closed my book before putting it away for the day. I stood up from the chair at the desk and walked to the window. Outside looked gloomy and cold. The girls were still sleeping as were the younger boys. Malinda and her father were also still sleeping too. However, I knew Elizabeth was up and down stairs. I walked out of the room to head down. Once there I could smell the aroma of coffee being made.

"Morning," I say to Elizabeth and Molly. Those two have really made a friendship. Elizabeth has learned so much on cooking from her. I as well but not much because Molly always has me keep the children with company.

"Morning," Molly says with a smile as she purses a cup of coffee and hands it to me. I sit across from Elizabeth at the little table in the kitchen. Molly opens up the oven door and pulls out a pot. She grabbed three dinner rolls and sets them on the table. Then she puts the pot back in the oven. The rolls were left over from last night's supper. It was alright for it being duck and noodles.

"Since it's us three that are the only ones up I thought we could finish these rolls up before we start feeding and cooking," Molly said coming over and sitting down with the small dish with butter. We each grabbed one and past the knife around after we were done buttering our roll up.

"So Elizabeth, how old are you," Molly asked. Elizabeth swallowed her sip of coffee and said with a smile on her beautiful face, "I'm eighteen."

"Oh then and so that means you're older than Katherine?"

"Indeed, she is," I budded in, and we start to giggle. I just hope that this birthday in this house hold won't end up like the last one. I really mean it for Elizabeth and Eric.

Mid afternoon and Elizabeth, Molly, and I are fixing super. We decided to switch things up. We were going to have an earlier supper and no dinner. Molly and Elizabeth want to cook one more meal this afternoon. The family didn't argue over that. During our meal before we ate we prayed and passed everything around. This supper was an average talking supper. Like the usual, it was Justin, John, and Malinda talking together. The younger children would talk to each other. Molly, Elizabeth, and Eric would talk to each other while I would stare and listen once in a while. I was only eating. That's all I ever do is eat and sleep and do my chores. I talk very few to everyone.

After supper, I move to the sofa to sit and watch everyone. We all move and go our separate ways like usual. Elizabeth still sits at the table with a bright smile on her face. Molly comes in holding a cake in a pan and places it in front of her. Almost everyone moves back to the table while Molly is slicing a piece for everyone. Then Elizabeth would hand them out from where she was sitting. I didn't bother to get up and eat some cake. I wasn't in the mood. I wasn't in the mood to be happy for her coming of age.

I haven't been in the cheery mood for a while. Every day I drown myself in sadness and memories. I refuse to look at them. When I see them that one memory appears, and it stays there until I can get my mind off of it. I clench my fist. I watch the younger children play with their dolls and soldiers. They all found out days later and have not talked to me much. Maybe they have tried, and I've just been ignoring them. I don't want to I love and care for them too much.

I would have to switch passions from sitting too long in one area. Move one leg over the other while stretching out my back. I just sit here, and watch time move on. Eric comes and sits down next to me with a smile on his face. I ignore his gaze and watch the children play. From the corner of my eye, I see him leaning in closer towards my ear.

"Katherine," he whispers. Still not looking I get up to make my way to the kitchen. No one was in there. Eric gets up and fallows me. We stop as I face the wood-burning stove. I can feel that he is staring at me. He walks up steadily from the sound of the floor cracking. His hands slowly come up to my arms then to my shoulders. Then suddenly he jerks me around, and we are personally close. My eyes water up as my lip curls under a few times.

"Katherine," he whispered again.

"I'm sorry I just can't!" I say and shove him out of the way.

…

Thanksgiving Day and Molly, Elizabeth, and I had to get up extra early to prepare for the one meal we are making today. Molly has told Elizabeth and me for days now we are only going to cook one meal today. Molly's and Justin's family are coming up. We've received word from neighbors saying they came in sometime during the week and have been staying in town. Elizabeth and I have only met Molly's side of the family but not Justin's. I hope he doesn't have a niece who is stubborn like Natalie was back in July.

I would have to say that it is maybe six in the morning. We all honestly don't get up until about seven at the earliest. Yesterday we were so thankful that the boys got a turkey, and we were actually lucky because they got two. They were both small birds, but they'll still feed this family.

We had this day planned. Molly even said to us that she was thankful for Elizabeth and I to show up in this family, just so she could have some more help. In the kitchen, I was getting all of our coffees ready for us. Cooking today will get my mind off of everything and everyone. And again Ethan and I have not talked once since the day we split. And also with his family coming over it's going to make things a little more awkward.

It's been nearly a month currently. And yes, I doubt myself. I feel confused about this between us. I hate but still miss him. I want my mama to be here to help me. I miss my mama.

Love doesn't come through time.

Chapter 18

December is here, and snow has been falling for the last few days. It will fall one day then the following day it would all melt and fall again the next. The weather just has a mind to its own. I watch the snow fall from sitting on the porch swing. Yes, it is crazy of me sitting out here when it is snowing, and it being cold, but I have a blanket around me with my coat on. I have my boots with my stockings on under.

When living in the city mama, and I would just sit out on our porch and watch the city life move before our eyes. We would have our coffee in our hands to warm them up, so they don't get cold. I remember we would be talking about different things. We would laugh and cry and even once we got into a fight. I miss that. Father would get so mad at us for staying out in the cold like that, but we didn't care. We would only stay outside for maybe a few minutes, and that's it. Because after that we would go inside to pure, more coffee into our cups and snuggle up by the fire with a blanket around us and read.

However, living out here in the country it makes it more beautiful. I love how the snow makes a blanket for the cold dry ground. You can see only the tips of the grass showing just a bit. The snow is falling harder this evening more than what it was this morning. Off in the distend, I see

Ethan cutting fire wood by the barn. He would cut three or four in a row and then look up at me whipping down his face.

The front door open fast and Molly walks out of the house with her eyes narrowed. She stands there with a shawl wrapped around her then saying, "Katherine Stone what are you doing out here in this weather?" I jump up and start walking fast to get inside.

"Don't you know that it's cold outside, and you could get sick? My lord girl what's gotten into you?" she asked while closing the door. I try my best not to say anything and head straight up stairs, but she stops me.

"Wait. Hold on, don't go. Come right here missy." I stop to turn around and sit in the chair she has out for me in the kitchen. She purses me a cup of coffee.

"What were you doing out there sitting in the cold?" she asked sitting down drinking her coffee. I sit there with a smile on my face.

"I was trying to feel Molly," I said putting my cup on the table and then scooting my chair closer towards her. Molly sits there gazing at me with a look thinking I was stupid.

"You were what?" It was only us in the kitchen. Everyone else was either in the family room, upstairs, or out in the barn.

"I was trying to feel something. Back home my mama and I would do this all the time when it would snow." I started to say while she stares at me still. "Father would get so mad at us, but we didn't care. We only knew that we were doing something that we loved to do together." I was smiling even harder now.

"Katherine I believe you have a fever. Now go up stairs and lay down."

"But," I started to say. "No buts go!" she raised her voice and went over to check on the dinner rolls in the wood-burning stove. I started to walk up stairs and got in bed to lie down.

...

Two days have gone by, and Molly was right because I did have a fever. I'm getting better now but slowly. Molly is making me stay in bed for only one more day if I get better by then. And I believe I will. I lie on my side and watch the door. I got tired of staring at the floor. The family doesn't have any more books because I've read them all! They only had a few and with them; I have had the children read out loud to me in privet.

Samuel and Jeffery don't like reading out loud and so didn't Marty. Emma, Madison, and Savanna don't really care if they have to read out loud or not. They just like it because they are learning.

My door opens up slowly. I don't know what time it is because I would doze off to sleep every so often. A face appears and its Ethan. The one face next to Malinda I don't want to see.

"How are you?" he asked just standing in front of the door not moving any closer.

"No I'm not talking to you," I say my voice soft. I sit up just a little.

"Katherine just hear me out; I don't want to cause any trouble between us." He would say sliding his boots on the floor.

"Katherine," he said then the door slams open and Eric comes in.

"Ethan I think you should leave?" Eric asked his brother showing the way out. The brothers stare each other down. Then without words being spoken from Eric, Ethan leaves the room. Eric closes the door and walks over towards me to sit down on the bed. He comes in and hugs me tight. I was not crying there was no need for me to cry because I wasn't sad from what had just happened.

"Are you okay? Elizabeth and I have been trying our best for that situation to never happen."

"Eric I'm fine. And maybe things like that should happen. I can't keep ignoring him forever we still live under the same ruff." I said and then he leaves the room. Eric is like an older brother to me. I really feel that he, and Elizabeth are going to get married one of these days. I also felt that way about Ethan and me but I just never said anything. That's because I thought, we were going to last longer of courting. I'm bored and lonely. I hate being sick. I just want my mama and only her.

It's Christmas Eve night, and the family is all settled down for the night. We ate ham and had mashed potatoes. We dressed up nice for once other than church. And now we go to bed and sleep and wait for what tomorrow will bring us.

Christmas morning and all the younger children come bursting into my room. They all started to jump on the bed waking Elizabeth and I up.

"Wake up its Christmas day!" Samuel cheered. "Elizabeth, wake up!" Emma said forcing her to get out of the warm bed.

"Go wake up your brother!" Elizabeth smiled making a joke. Then suddenly the children started to run towards the door. "And make lots of noise!" she yelled. Elizabeth was happy this morning and so was I. Well, I'm going to try to be. I get up and get dressed. I put on my little blue blouse with my light-brown skirt. Elizabeth gets out her dark-blue blouse with her yellow skirt. We fix our hairs up nice. Well, she does. I decided to leave mine down for the day.

When we walk down stairs, I hear Malinda and her father talking in their room. Once down stairs, I see the tree up and decorated with few presents under it. After breakfast, we got to open up our presents. We all sat down in a circle taking our turns to open our presents. All the girls got a brand new dress each. Samuel and Jeffery got new pants and a coat. Elizabeth got shoes as so did I. We knew that Molly was going to get us shoes. She asked a long time ago back in early November. Malinda got more things than all of us. Each one of us younger kids all got one present while she got nine or ten. Her father got all of these things for her. Malinda gets whatever she wants. Even back at home I would get maybe five or so presents from my parents. That's it. And even then I never asked for much.

I really would not ask for much at all. My father would just give me things if I said I wanted it or not. My father really never knew me like how mama does. That's why I always say, I miss mama. I miss her now.

Now that it is winter, and our day light is shorter we stop with the whole super and just have a late dinner. I've said something like this before but now Molly has changed things around. Molly, Elizabeth, and I head to the kitchen to prepare for dinner. Just this early morning the men shot down a beautiful turkey for dinner. He was big, round, and plumped. He was a beauty. Molly had me peel and mash the potatoes while Elizabeth kept an eye out for the rolls, so they don't burn and get too hard. Molly was on turkey duty. This time she was also having the girls watch and help. She has wanted them to watch and help even before Elizabeth, and I have arrived here. Molly had Marty and Savanna working on the pie and Emma and Madison was working on another pie. We were going to have pumpkin.

Then once it was time for dinner, we all sat down in the identical seats as we did the day of Eric's birthday. I realize that we have been sitting in these same seats since that day, and we have moved every so often. Before passing the dishes around Justin stood up and started to say, "I just want to say how much I love my friends and family here with me this Christmas. How much we have grown and changed." He just kept on going. Saying what he wanted to say not knowing if he really means it or not. Our dinner was getting cold. "And finely we should pray," he said bowing his head. He led off by starting.

Justin started to carve the turkey and was passing out the plates that he had down by him. He would carve a few slices and placed them on the plates. Then everyone would pass the plates down. After that we started to pass the dishes around the table. I started with the mashed potatoes that I prepared earlier this evening. While Marty had the rolls clear down on the other end. I didn't want to care who was here and where we are sitting. Today is Christmas Day and I was hungry and wanted to eat. I would look down at my plate staring at my turkey watching it as I chew. Then look up for once and see what we are talking about. Molly would talk to her four beautiful daughters as Elizabeth would talk to Eric, who would talk to his brothers. Madison would sometimes talk to me. Marty occasionally doesn't talk much either. I see that now.

I ask for the butter to butter my roll. This dinner was the best Christmas dinner I have ever had. I believe I did really well with preparing the potatoes! I'm proud of myself. Now I just stare at my half-empty plate and think of my family. I stab my fork into my turkey and shoved it into my mouth and start to chew. I think of how my grandma on my mama's side of the family constantly comes. Grandma would always walk in the door and the first thing she would say was, "I made cake!" She passed away late January of this year. I stop eating to take a drink of my water.

Everybody was already having seconds of what was left. During the non holidays we never would have enough for seconds. That was during the summer. However, with Malinda and her father we barely got enough now. After dinner Molly had all the girls help her wash the dishes. I sit on the sofa with Eric on my right and Elizabeth on his right. The boys were sitting by the fire watching Ethan stack some more wood in it. John and Justin were standing next to the fire place talking. Malinda was sitting in the other chair watching Ethan. She gives off this smile. Every smile she has is a, 'I want something now,' smile. Justin leaves the room and walks outside. John stays put talking to the younger boys. He would talk to them about having a plantation. However, Samuel and Jeffery didn't care to listen to him talk about that. They were young and still learning new things.

All four girls walk in the room and sit. Marty and Savanna sit on the floor while Emma and Madison were sitting on the chairs. I don't talk but just watch and listen. Later, Justin walks on in the house with an old white sack hanging behind his back.

"I found more presents left by the barn. I'm not sure who these belong to, but I'm guessing you?" he said placing the sack down in the middle of the family room. The children gather around. Marty opens that sack up and found a doll's house built. The girl's cheer and smile as their father got it out for them. Sam and Jeff look in and find some more soldiers that were carved out of small logs made for them.

I could see on their faces that they appreciated what their father has done for them. Molly slowly comes walking in and hands us bigger kids a paper that was folded. We all open the folded paper up to find some money.

"Oh Molly you shouldn't have," Elizabeth says tearing up.

"Mama, where did you get this money? You know you and pa need it more than us?" Eric says standing up and hugging his mother. All four of us tried giving our money to Molly, but she refused to take it back.

"Children please I have been saving that money for all of you so that you could have some. You could at least save it for a house. I'm sure you all are going to need money to buy a house and tend a farm." She was getting angry with us. She stared at the cold floor.

"Thank you," I say under my breath. Molly looks up with a cricket smile.

"Katherine may I see you in the kitchen?" Molly asked me. I stare at her and say, "Yes." I follow her until we stop in front of the cabinet. I watch her as she moves some plates and bowls. Then she reaches out another folded up paper.

"Katherine, this was sent in the mail to you," she pauses lowering her voice. "This was sent back at the beginning of October." Then she hands me my mail and leaves. I sit down at the table. There was only one thing that came in through my mind; this was a letter from my mama. I slowly open the seal and read.

Dear, my beloved daughter Katherine,

I got your letter, and I'm so proud of you and Elizabeth for finding a place to stay. Out of Elizabeth's parents and your father, I have been the only one worried about your safety. Your father doesn't talk anymore but only to Elizabeth's father. And even with her mother she talks to her friends. Katherine they are blaming me for you two leaving. I get pity from them.

Just the other day your father beat me. I have a bruise on my left side of my stomach. He even beats all the house maids. Now when we all cook for him if he doesn't like it, he'll throw his plate onto the floor. Then he'll make me clean it up. Daughter we all have bruises from him, if you could please come home. The two men you and Elizabeth were to marry they are still here. Your father thought he could find you. He is still looking for you. So if you two decide not to come back home, I understand.

Katherine I love you and Elizabeth. I just hope that one day we'll be together again. That's all I want is to be with my family. Your father doesn't love you. He has said it many of the times. He and Elizabeth's father both say that. Katherine even Elizabeth's mother says she doesn't love her. This is why I get pity from all of them. Your father isn't a good man. He never was and never will be. Someday it will just be me, you, and Elizabeth living together one day. Be safe daughter. Let Elizabeth know that I love her too.

Love mama

...

I cried. I held a hold of this letter then dropped it on the table. I cried harder and then ran out of the door. I become stiff from the blast of cold running through my body. I run to the barn, there it would be warmer for me to cry. I didn't bother to grab a coat or a shawl. My tears were cold to the touch on my cheek. Once in the barn, I close the door and climb in the back of the wagon. I hid my face. It wasn't but no more than a minute until the barn door opens and my name is called out, "Katherine?"

I didn't say anything. I knew who it was. It was Ethan. "Katherine, what are you doing out here, it's cold?" he asked with a furious voice. Are you angry with me?

"I wanted to get away," I answered. He climbs up on in the wagon with me. He sat in front of me staring at me as I did the same.

"Here take this." He hands me a coat. It wasn't mine but maybe one of Molly's or Elizabeth's.

"No I don't want it," I say arguing with him.

"Katherine you are a stubborn girl! Now can you please tell me why you ran out of the house crying?" he asked. Should I tell him what is happening back home? No I shouldn't because we have our differences.

"I can't tell you!" I cried out. He comes in closer and holds me. "I don't see why?" he asked but I push him away saying, "I don't need your sympathy." I get out of the back of the wagon. He follows as he keeps a hold of the coat. The barn creaks as the wind outside blows. The animal's inside sleep as it is almost sundown. I look away from Ethan as I can feel that he is watching me. I run my hands up on my arms to warm them up.

"It's my family again," I started to say. I didn't want it to but it just sort of slipped out. "My father has been beating my mama for a while." He slowly walks up behind me as I could hear his feet dragging on the dirt floor.

"And how do you know this?" he asks in a stern voice.

"Back in the summer I wrote to my mama to tell her that Elizabeth, and I had found a safe place to stay. It wasn't until October, I got the letter, but Molly kept it hidden from me. And now I don't know if this is still going on?"

"Is he still doing this? I'll go get Eric, and we'll all leave to get your mama. Come on," he said almost leaving the barn.

"Ethan," I yell out to him so that he'll stop to turn around to look at me. "You see I don't know if he is still doing this? And you don't know my father. He is constantly angry, and he has always put his anger out on us. It was always with me, but now I see he has moved it onto my mama. There is no helping her; we just can't." I turn away again to hold my hand over my mouth. He walks up to me.

"Katherine, it's okay," he says then rapping the coat around my shoulders. I turn around quick pushing him back saying, "Don't you see? It's not okay. It never will be! Why can't you understand that, Ethan?"

"You know Katherine; I don't understand? I don't understand how you treat me like this. How I will always be there for you, and yet you don't want me!" he yelled.

"It all leads back to that day, that one day," I say waving my arms out.

"You're still on that day? It was months ago!" He backs up away.

"It was months ago and it still hurts to know that, Ethan!" I say. Ethan bends down to pick up a small hand full of straw. Then he looks at me with a cricket smile. He was up to something? He would walk closer again.

"Look Katherine, I'm sorry."

"No Ethan, you're not!" I cried. His face was truing soft by his eyes. He looked to be almost crying.

"I love you, Katherine. I thought I didn't but I still do," He would wipe his face around his eyes so often.

"I gave myself to you Ethan a long time ago and now look at us?" I say. I feel this could be going somewhere. I run my hands up against the sides of my arms to warm them. The wind would blow a cool crisp air into the small opening of the barn door. Ethan walked closer towards me.

"I have straw so kiss me just once," he asked from me while holding the straw above both our heads. I stare at him narrowing my eye brows.

"No Ethan I won't kiss you," I say. This was stupid. But yet he leaned in closer. I could feel his warm breath above my chapped cold lips. Just the smell I smell from him makes me want to kiss him. However, I can't I just won't. He leans in closer. Our lips are just hovering over each other's. Oh how I love the warmth. Then I wrap my arms around his neck as he wrapped his arms against the middle section of my back. We both gave in on this.

I leaned my head back and opened my eyes wide.

"I'm sorry but we just can't," I say then backing up. However, I couldn't because he grabbed a hold upon my arm and squeezed it hard.

"Katherine, don't you remember that I gave myself to you too?" He asked. My face was getting cold to the touch and turning red from the cold. I couldn't bear this anymore.

"I do remember Ethan but we can't do this, not after you betrayed me like that months ago. And I'm not sorry for it either. You should find out who is?" I say then I ran out of the barn and up to the house. I was hoping he wasn't going to run after me, and he didn't. Once in the house I hang whose coat I had on and head up to my room for bed. I was done talking to everyone about everything. I just want to see my mama and have her hold me.

...

December 29, 1860 and I turn the age of eighteen. I told Molly that I would be okay with just a cake and for her to read to me a little from my bible. I wanted this because I have been feeling alone lately. I know I have this family here with me, but it's not all of my family. Things between Ethan and I have been a little awkward since we kissed once more again on Christmas night. We haven't talked since then.

…

Two days go by and it's December 31, 1860. The last day of the year before 1861 comes. We sit all around the table again having our New Years Eve's dinner. John brought in some Champaign and whisky for us to drink. Justin cracks open both bottles and start to pour them both into glasses. We women drank the Champaign as the men drank the whisky. After a few hours had gone by some of us were getting a little drunk. We would stand up and be dizzy, and we'd slur our words. However, that was only with the men and Malinda. She really likes her Champaign. I just started my second glass. It was almost midnight. Most of the boys were in bed. They don't like to stay up late.

"Friends, Family I have something to say before the new coming of the year. Ethan you are going to love this!" John laughs while he's drunk. "Oh Ethan you are like a son to me. You always have been."

"What about me John?" Eric says stumbling up. He too is a little drunk. The family laughs as he said that.

"Eric, sit down!" Molly whispers at him. Eric turns to his mother smiles and sits down slowly. Elizabeth has to nearly force him down.

"Any ways back to me talking Ethan my son," John said. Ethan just stairs at him with a half smile. "The only other thing there is for me to say is that I am allowing you to marry my daughter!" Molly, Eric, Elizabeth, Ethan, and I sit there without saying a word. The girls just watch us. And during this whole time, Malinda is cheering to death.

"Oh father this is the best New Years present you have ever gotten me!" Malinda cheers and gets up and kisses Ethan hard on the lips in front of the family. Ethan with his eyes open forces her to get off but fails. Finally Malinda stops and gulps for air. Ethan whips his lips with an angry look on his face.

"Wait what?" he said standing up as the chair behind him falls back.

"Justin did you fail to tell your son that he is to marry my daughter?" John asked his friend Justin. Justin looks up nearly drunk and says, "You know what John, I did fail to tell my son that!"

"Ethan you and Malinda are to be wed."

"Justin is this true?" Molly stands up frustrated. "Yes Molly it is."

"Kitchen now!" she says pointing the way. "Molly we can talk in here. I already know that it's going to be about Malinda and Ethan. And they need to hear what we have to say." Justin was getting a temper by now. I was staring at Ethan as he was staring back at me. Eric got up and walked over to his brother and was trying to talk to him. However, Eric was too drunk to even stand up next to him. Ethan had to help him. Elizabeth was trying to talk to me, but I wasn't listening.

I was still staring at Ethan as he was doing the same. Since Christmas day, I finally think I, however, have feelings for him. And think he still does too. Of course, he still does he told me. And now with him getting married, I don't know what to do? I stood up to go to the kitchen and stood there in front of the burning fire to get warm. Molly comes in and stands next to me.

"Katherine," she says. It was all she said nothing after that. I feel angry and depressed but not really sure on the both.

"I want to go home," I said angry.

"Katherine I'm sorry but it's too cold for anyone to travel in this weather. If you want to go home you'll have to wait until spring when the snow melts." She whispers then leaves me to be.

"Katherine," a different voice calls out low. I know who it was; it was Ethan.

"What," I asked not turning around for him.

"Talk to me please. I need a friend. I need my love," he explains. I turn around to face him to say, "I am not your friend, nor your love!" I then walked pass him to head to the family room. I was done running to my room to cry and hide from the family. I went over to sit next to Elizabeth and Eric. They are my friends and love, not Ethan. Ethan is just a person in the back of my mind. He is no one. I bite my lip to help with no crying.

Chapter 19

January, February, and March have gone by. We made it through winter finally. I was getting cabin fever from always having to stay in the house. However, once when the snow finally melted, and we could see the sun shining, the girls and I would go outside and play. But yet we are still suck in the house. Because from March through May and a little of June all it does is rain.

It's a warm sunny April morning. The family had to get up early for church this morning. We were all ready and waiting for the men to bring up the wagon. We leave to go to church down the dusty road. We go to church every Sunday, but I still don't know how to get there. Plus during winter, we couldn't leave the property. This morning is the first morning we got to leave the house. It feels so good to see the town. To look at how everyone has changed even though I don't know anyone from here.

When we made it to the church all of us, kids would jump down in the back of the wagon. Ethan rode up with Malinda and her father in their wagon. Throughout winter, we haven't talked to each other. Once in a while we would say something like "Will you pass the rolls down or your mother needs more wood." That was it basically. Eric sometimes talks for us. He would talk for us a lot to be honest.

Walking in the church I look around. It's small, but I feel a big welcome coming in. We make our way to sit down. Marty was at the end next to the aisle. Elizabeth and Eric and the rest of the family were sitting on my left. Ethan was sitting next to the aisle on the other side. He was sitting next to Malinda and her father.

The people in the church started to quiet down once Father stood up in front to speak.

"Good morning," he'd say waving his arms out. We all just sit here staring at him up front.

"I see that we all survived the winter just fine." Everybody started to laugh a little. A little into the session we would start to sing and read along. I hope the girls are reading along from what I taught them during the winter. I'm sure they are. While singing through one song, I glanced over my right to see Ethan. He would sing and then glance over at me. Knowing me I did the stupid thing and looked away then after a while I'd look back at him. He was still staring at me.

What's weird was that he smiled at me. Or he smiled at someone else in front of me a few rows up. I'd stand up a little farther to try to see over everyone's heads but nothing. No one else was looking back at him. After singing for the second time we got to sit back down. I lean back in my seat and listen along. I picture his smile again in my mind. Warm? No. Cold, no a smile can't be cold. Wait I take that back. After that I have nothing to say about that. Maybe he saw me looking at him and then the first thought was to smile back? Either way I really won't know the truth.

We finally got through all of church. Afterward, everyone was talking outside to see how we all survived the harsh winter. I stand outside all alone watching everyone talk. I move my hand over my eyes to block the sun. Molly walks up to me with a smile on her face.

"We'll be here for a little while talking. So you could go talk to our neighbors or just sit inside with the boys and their friends," she says then yells out her one friends name to go and hug her. I look behind me to see Samuel and Jeffery inside sitting talking to their friends. I didn't want to sit and wait. So I think I'll go and take a stroll around where ever I feel like going. I'd look back behind me to see if I was being followed, and I wasn't.

Once when I got to a tree, I'd touch its bark to feel the roughness of it. I miss the feeling of spring. I miss seeing the grass turning to its natural color and the bird's singing. After walking a few more feet I start to hear someone walking up behind me. I turn around to see Ethan walking pass the tree I touched. I walk around a tree with a smile on my face asking, "What are you doing here?" Ethan runs his hand through his hair saying with a smile on his face, "I saw you walking and wanted to check on you. Are you okay?"

He follows me around the tree.

"Oh, I'm okay Ethan. You don't need to be check on me, only if you hear any screaming for help!" I teased. This has been the second time we have talked.

"May I walk with you?" he asked. I wanted to say no, but I don't want an awkward situation between us again.

"Yes you may," I say, and we start to walk. We would talk for a little while and then there would be a dead silence. The past few months have changed us. It's like we are getting to know each other all over again. Perhaps it's good? Or perhaps that's bad?

We got to a stop in front of a tree. I look at it and started thinking about climbing it. It was low enough for me to climb. I knew Ethan wouldn't like me to climb it, but that's why I'm going to do it. I reach out to place my foot down on a branch then I'd pull myself up.

"Katherine what do you think you're doing?" He'd asked.

"What does it look like I'm doing, I'm climbing a tree," I said. I'd step onto another branch. After I found a strong enough branch, I'd then place my butt onto it to sit. Ethan was looking up at me. I really wasn't that far from the ground. His head could be about waist high to me if he came closer.

"Katherine I want you to come down from there," he asked.

"And why?" I played around.

"Because you could fall and get hurt," he said then touching my knee. A tingle went through my body.

"You're going to have to make me come down," I demanded. Then I grabbed a hold of another branch and stood up. Ethan walks away saying, "I know you Katherine; you're stubborn."

"Oh and how do you know that?" I asked. As he was walking away I could feel that the bottom branch was shaking a little.

"Ah Ethan," I called out not loudly, but he didn't hear me. He was too busy talking about how stubborn I am.

"No listen Katherine from the time we haven't been together I have learned more about you. How you act around ones you love and how you act…" The branch was shaking even more.

"Ethan," I yelled. He looks back running towards me saying, "Katherine!"

I grab a hold of the top branch with my arms lifting my upper body. My feet dangle. The bottom branch broke and fell to the ground. Ethan stands there with his arms out.

"Jump down I'll catch you," he says.

"Are you kidding me?" I laughed sort of. My arms were getting tired.

"Yes let go and no, I'm not kidding you." I looked at him and said, "Here I come." I let go and as he caught me. We both fell to the ground. As we fell we rolled around but this time I was on the ground, and he was on top of me.

"Are you okay?" he asked me. We looked into each other's eyes. I think this is silly, but I sure am feeling something between us.

"Yes I'm okay, are you?"

"I am if only you are."

"Ethan," I started to say then breathing.

"Yes Katherine," I could see my face in his big brown eyes. I missed those eyes.

"Are you feeling the same thing as I am between us?" I said.

"I was just about to say the same thing to you."

Then out of know where he leaned in, and we started to kiss. I gave into quick and started to kiss back even harder. We would roll around in the grass with our hands on the backs of each other's heads. I wonder if he, however, loves me. Of course, I think he still does because we are kissing. He then started to kiss down my neck.

"Ethan," I started to say as he mounded.

"Ethan, wait." He then lifted his head.

"What are we doing?" I asked. He was still lying on top of me.

"What do you mean?" I gave him a look. He then sat up off of me.

"I mean you're going to be getting married in a few weeks, and you're here kissing me like your still in love with me?"

He scratched his head and held my hand.

"Katherine I am still in love with you," He said out in the open. He didn't hesitate at all which I like. I stood up to lean against the tree. He leaned his arm just above my head and leaned in close to me with a cricket smile.

"I'm so glad you said that!" I smiled.

"Why," he asked needing to know why I said that.

"Because Ethan I still love you too," I say looking away with my hair covering my face. He leaned in closer. I knew this because his breathing was moving my hair. Then his fingers came in from under to move my hair out of my face and to move my head back to face his to kiss me slowly. In between kisses, He would say, "I... love... that... you... said... that..." I missed the kissing and passion we had for each other. But yet I still wonder about the wedding?

"Wait Ethan, what about the wedding," I asked. He looked up at me.

"I'll think of something soon," He hesitated. I just smile. After a few more minutes of kissing, we leave the tree to walk back to the church. He went one way as I did the same to make it seem that we didn't see each other at the same time in the woods. We know that it could or could not work.

The way home was quiet. I had a smile generally the whole time with butterflies in my stomach. And yet no one asked why I was smiling. Once at home Ethan and I kept our distends like normal just to make it not seem like we were back together even though I want to be with him.

. . .

It's the middle of May, and I ran out of paper in my diary. So I have to keep my thoughts in my head. Ethan and I would see each other in the barn loft like the first time we spent together just about a year ago. I remember that day so well. It was the first time since Elizabeth, and I left home. Or that happened a few days after words? And that night Ethan and I had our first kiss together. However, that happened in July.

John and Malinda are still planning the wedding. I keep on reminding Ethan to stop it, but he hasn't done anything about it. And it's making me mad. I don't know how else to tell him without making him angry at me. Ethan and I were standing out back beside the barn to have some privacy. I would be leaning against the barn as he would have his hands down by my hips, and then he would be kissing my neck. It was just about sundown, and it looked beautiful. The clouds were a prefect pink, orange, and gray color. There was no wind blowing.

"Ethan you know you have less than two weeks before your soon to be wedding," I mention to him. He lifts up his head and gives me a death stare. He walks back moving his hands just behind his head.

"Oh Katherine you just had to ruin the moment?" he asked then laughing sarcastically.

"Well have you done anything to help?"

"No Katherine I haven't," he says. I start to get angry. All I just want him to do is to stop what shouldn't be happening.

"Why is it so important for you to know if I have or haven't said anything yet," he yelled.

"Because I love you," I sighed.

"Katherine I love you too, but what if this can't work out," he asked. I then looked up.

"Then we'll run away." I said. He looks me in the eyes. The sunset was making it hard for me to see his beautiful face.

"Katherine, that could work!" he says.

"Really," I asked.

"No it won't work damn it!" he yells.

"What are you saying Ethan I thought that would work?" I asked I was getting confused with what he wanted me to understand. He just said yes and then he said no?

"Katherine, aren't you done running?" he asked.

"Yes I am," I say moving my hands over my heart.

"Well, you see I don't want to run," he said.

"So what does this mean again," I asked.

"This means we're through, and I'll marry Malinda like planned. I just want you to know Katherine," he posed. He was standing there close to me staring at me with those big brown eyes. They were burning a hole in my heart. It was breaking apart and turning into ashes.

"I will constantly still love you no matter what; I will always," then he leans in order to kiss my forehead and walks away. I fall to the ground and sigh out loud while watching him walk away into the sunset. I couldn't believe this once more. Ethan was leaving me again.

Chapter 20

The date June 1 and the family were getting ready to leave for the wedding. The men left mid yesterday to already be at the church this morning. Molly would help with the girls getting ready as I would just watch. Elizabeth would help also. Malinda was downstairs eating or something. I really didn't care what she was doing. Malinda didn't have Ethan's sister in the wedding but yet not even any of her friends. I believe it's because she doesn't have any friends. All four girls had their hair braided back. Elizabeth and I had to help.

"Katherine, are you sure you don't want to come?" Molly asked putting her hand on my shoulder. She was staring me down.

"No," I murmured staring at the floor then looking up at her. She smiles and walks away with her family behind. I eventually walked down with them. The girls all sat down in the family room talking. I see Malinda standing in the kitchen with her purple dress on staring at her wedding dress that is hanging on the wall. She had both her hands on her hips before turning around and seeing me standing there.

"Malinda, are you ready? If so I'll go and hook up the horses to the wagon," Molly said and then started walking out the door.

"Yes Molly I am!" Malinda said as Molly walked out. No one has eaten yet this morning. I went over to the pot on the stove to check it. I see that there are a few biscuits left from yesterday morning. I grab all of them and place them on the table and hunt through the cabinets to find the honey. I call for the girls to come and get their breakfast. Elizabeth later comes down and heads outside to help Molly; I'm guessing?

Malinda still stands there watching her dress with her hands on her hips. All the girls go and eat at the dining table as I eat at the table in the kitchen. Elizabeth comes in grabs Malinda's dress.

"What do you think you're doing?" Malinda asked tugging at her dress.

"Molly asked for me to take it for you. Come on girls your mama is almost ready!" Elizabeth yells afterwards. She leaves with the dress, and the girls fallowing behind. I sit here at the table staring at Malinda.

"Well Katherine," she starts to say facing me while still standing. "I'm living the dream, your dream!" She pointed at me.

"What are you saying Malinda?" I ask taking a sip from my coffee that I got earlier just now.

"I've been planning this day for years since that first day I met Ethan. I knew my father was going to make us get married. And once we're married; we're heading down to Georgia to live and raise a family." She would say walking back in forth.

"You know I really don't care what you're saying about all of this," I said.

"You know Katherine; I never did like you? I knew you were with Ethan at that moment I arrived here," she paused. "Back in August my father had received a letter from Justin saying that Ethan was in love with a girl who moved in. I had to act fast on having my father take me here."

"Where are you going with all of this Malinda?" I asked. I stopped eating and stared at her. She lifted an eye brow. I stood up to face her.

"I still don't care!" I said loud for her to hear me correctly. She just stands there frozen.

"I'm glad you're not coming to our wedding," she laughs. I clench my hand. Elizabeth comes in through the door saying, "Malinda we're ready, are you?"

"Yes Elizabeth I am." Then Malinda turns around and starts heading out the door. I wait for a while until I saw them pull out of the drive. Then

I run straight to my room crying. Instead, I ran into Ethan's room and onto his bed. I keep telling myself that I don't love him, and I still don't know if that's true or not? It's too late for us to get together still. His bed smelled like him, all of his blankets and one pillow. It wasn't a good smell from after every working day, he would be all sweaty, but it was his smell. I was getting his pillow wet from my tears. Is this love? No it can't be?

I slow my breathing down and try to calm myself. My eyes were getting heavy, and I was about to fall asleep. The first face that pops into my mind is Ethan.

...

Ethan stands there in a summer haze. The air was warm from the sun shining down on us. We were out back by the side of the barn talking. We would move to the barn walls to sit next to it.

"I love you," he says out in the open. I smile at him saying, "You do!" We sit there facing each other.

"Yes I truly do!" he laughs. He slowly brings his hands closer to mine wanting to hold them. I yank them back saying with a stern voice, "Prove it?"

"What?"

"Prove to me that you love me! What is it that you love about me?" I demanded!

"I love your eyes, noise, smile, laugh, and most of all your heart for mine," he answered with a slow smooth voice.

"What do you mean your heart for mine?" I asked. I would move my hair of what came out of my braid out of my face. He too moved some hair out from above his eyes.

"I know you Katherine. You love me too, and you're just as well scared to say it to me. So that is why I am saying it for you," he explained. My eyes lit up, and a smile appeared across my face.

And yet his brown eyes became darker. His smile was fading. His glow was darkening. He was becoming dark. He was fading from me. Ethan was leaving my sight without even getting up and walking away?

"Ethan," I yelled for him.

"Ethan I..."

...

"Ethan I love…" I yelled waking up. I knew I had fallen asleep. I didn't know what time it was to know how long I was sleeping. Or maybe I need to know what day it is?

"I love you Ethan," I said to myself out loud so that I could really hear myself say it. "No I don't? Oh Lord please tell me if I do or not?" I run to my room to find my bible. I know I grew up not knowing one thing to another about the bible, but if I just read it, perhaps, just perhaps it will tell me something. Maybe I can find my answer in there. I jump out of Ethan's bed and run to my room. I scrambled around the room to find the book.

"Damn it!" I would say out loud. I started to throw things out of my way. I didn't care whose stuff it was? I was determined to find that bible. "Where is it?" I yelled.

"Oh how could this have happened between us?" I looked under my bed then on top of it, but nothing? My hair kept on getting in my way. I had to take it out of its braid. I stopped looking. I was getting too mad at this all. I mean do I love him? Could I really still love him after all that he has done to me? Could the bible give me the answer? I fall to my knees and hide my face in my arms on the bed.

"Lord help me. I need to know do I love him. Does he love me?" I asked out loud crying.

"Ethan, oh do I love you? Do you love me? Do I love you? Do I love…? I love you," I stopped saying then raising my head. I dried my eyes, "I love Ethan!" I stood up to leave my room.

"The wedding I think I still have time to stop it!" I yelled running down the stairs. I ran out the door to the front house. Once in the drive I nearly tripped from my boots. I slammed the barn door open. I saw that there was Roller which was left here. He was my only quick way to get to the church.

I unhook him from his post and grabbed a blanket to throw on top of him. I next jump onto him yelling, "Y'all!" He makes a noise then I directed him to the right way to the church. The family has been going to this church for a long time. However, since Elizabeth and I have lived here on the way to the church we have always been sitting in the back. So I really have no clue where the church is at? I never realized how much I like riding! I love the feeling and the wind blowing through my hair! All I knew was that I was getting closer to town.

I've been going through my head what I should say. Should I say something? My heart is pounding. I keep losing my grip of the reins. I just now passed the second creek. I'm almost there. I can see the courthouse. Once in town, I stop Roller to ask someone where the church is located at.

"You sir, can you please direct me where the church is at?" I asked. He slowly takes off his hat and point saying, "Well miss you just take this road on straight. Then you would take a right at the first stop there by the old wind mill. That road will take you up on to the church. You can't miss it."

I pull the reins and yell, "Yes thank you!" I knew he said something after that, but I was too far away to hear, and I'm running out of time. I ride this road until I pass the wind mill.

"Oh shoot, I passed it!" I yelled. I turned around to head down the right road I was supposed to turn down on. This was taking too long. I feel that I am too late. What if they already both said I do? I was almost to the church. I can see the bells at the top.

Once I got there I had no place to tie Roller. I didn't have time too. I scrambled my way to get to the altar. Luckily, this was an outdoor wedding. It gave me more time to stop it. I slam the gate open as it makes a loud noise. Everyone looks back to see me. I see that Malinda just got up there where Ethan was standing. The wind blows as my hair still got in the way onto my face. Ethan looks back and sees me. He smiles as I smile. Malinda looks back with an angry smirk.

"Stop the wedding!" I yelled. I spotted Molly and Justin sitting in the very front. Molly stands up. Most of the people here are from Malinda's side of the family. I couldn't hear Ethan, but I knew he said something because Malinda turns to looking at him.

"Katherine," he yells then starts running to me.

"Ethan," I yell once more then start to run to him. Just half-way down the aisle I trip on my dress. I didn't pull it up in time as I was running.

"What are you doing here?" he asked. I stare into his big brown eyes. We smile.

"I love you!" I cheered. Everyone around us gasped.

"Katherine," he started to say.

"Katherine, don't you see I can't love you no more," he finally said. My smile disappeared. I stepped up close to him and slapped his face. He moves his hand over the raw mark I made. I wave my hand to slap him again until he stops and grabs my arm.

"I will not marry Malinda. I can't because I don't love her. I don't love anyone," he said. My heart broke into a million pieces.

"I only love Katherine," he says and then comes up and kisses me slowly. All I could hear around me was everyone gasping. Then I slapped him again to mean that I hate him for doing something that brilliant to me.

"I love you," I say while he is rubbing his face, and then he says, "I love you more than anything Katherine," after that we both wrap our arms around each other and kiss again.

Malinda then comes down the stairs yelling, "Pa?" Justin, Molly and John all came and surrounded us.

"Boy what is this none since?" John asked with an angry tone. Ethan stares at him then back at me. Malinda has an angry look on her face.

"No, none since no one wants to hear my side of the story. No one ever wants to hear my side of the story!" Ethan raised his voice.

"Well let's hear it then Ethan," Molly says with her voice calm. Ethan took a deep breath inside and let it out.

"A year ago to this day, Eric and I were in the general store. We were arguing about Malinda coming at some point in that later year. We both knew that Justin was going to have one of us married her. He has told us many of the times when we were younger but just not which one of us? I looked out the window and saw you staring in. I knew you couldn't see me from the way the sun was shining that evening. I saw you, and this crazy idea came through my mind that quick! I knew I have never seen you around town, so I knew you had to have been new to town. Eric and I were still arguing. As he was paying for his supplies, I saw that you were in the middle of the road and everyone outside was running. That's when I ran out to see and then saw that there was that wagon coming at you. So I just had to run after you to help you up! And at that moment when I saw your face, I knew you were the girl for me. You couldn't see my face from the sun shining. Then everyone was coming around so I had to tell them that you were okay. I wanted you. If you wouldn't have come and fell in the middle of the road this, here would be my wedding? Katherine I love you. I have since that day I saved you! That first glimpse with the sun shining making you glow from the general store. I love you and I always will! Katherine you're my window. I get to see all the different things that you bring out into the world for me."

He had a lot to say. A tear fell from the side of my cheek, and I laughed a little. It was so heartwarming to hear that from him.

"Justin you knew this ever since the boys were young?" Molly asked facing her husband. Justin stood their speech less.

"Yes dear I have. John and I knew that we were going to have this happen and that day is today," Justin explained.

"Oh dear Lord, please help me?" Molly says then walks away to sit with her daughters and to talk to others around her of what's going on probably.

"Pa what about me," Malinda complains to her father. None of us knew what will happen next with all of this.

"Son, what are you going to be doing?" Justin asked.

"Pa, I can't marry Malinda when my heart belongs to someone else."

"What are you saying son? This was your plan." Ethan stood closer to his father to stare him down.

"This was never my plan. You never knew what my plan was ever going to be!" Ethan says grinding his teeth. He then steps back looking at me around him at everyone else.

"There will not be a wedding today because I will not be marring Malinda! I'm not sure whether I will marry anyone today? However, I will marry someone later," he says then turns to me. We both walk up to each other holding hands together.

"Katherine Stone, I love you; I have always loved you since the very first. I want to marry you, and I want to marry you soon," he says. We smile, and both give out a cute little laugh together.

"This is an outrage!" John yells out swinging his arms.

"John I'm sorry that this can't happen, but I have idiot sons who won't listen to the best," Justin says.

"Justin I thought you were better than this. Now our friendship is over. The money is over. Come on Malinda, we're going home today!" John yells out and leaves the church yard getting lost in the maze of wagons.

"Go home everyone there's nothing to see here," Justin yells out then leaving the church yard also. Everyone who was not a part of the immediate family started to get up and leave. I never saw any of Molly's family here? Malinda and her father were responsible for who to invite and not.

Eric, Elizabeth, Ethan and I stand there in the middle of the aisle watching the crowd of people leave with a disgusting face. All four of us stand there smiling. Ethan and I were holding hands. After everyone who we all didn't know left someone tapped my shoulder. I turn around to see Molly with a smile on her face.

"Molly," I start to say.

"Katherine I have someone who wants to see you," she says then moving out of the way. I see a woman standing behind her. She had on a beautiful light blue dress. I then cover my mouth with my hands. I stopped breathing and started balling. There stood my mama that I haven't seen in a year.

"Mama," I asked her. She stands there with a bright smile on her face and crying.

"Yes Katherine, it's me!" she said. We then started walking towards each other hugging and crying harder than we both could. At this second, I couldn't believe that I would ever see my mama ever again.

"How is it that you're here?" I asked her through cries.

"I received an invite to the wedding," she cried. We stop hugging to see each other's faces. We would then wipe the tears off of each other's eyes. I didn't ask any questions on who sent the invite, I just knew it was Molly.

"Katherine I need to tell you something," she starts to say. I look back behind me to see everyone who was still here watching us.

"I left your father. I just walked out on him once I, received the invite a few months back. I've been staying at the hotel here in town. Molly has been helping me. She's a really nice lady and will be a very good mother in law for you!" she says smiling. We turn around and hug again; I stare at Molly and say 'thank you' to Molly with my lips no words. Molly smiles at me.

"Mama," Elizabeth cried out to my mama and went to hug her and cry. I walk over to Ethan, and we wrap our arms around each other and smile.

"Ma'am," he says to her with a smile as mama smiles back at him and then they both hug.

...

June 2, 1861 late evening the next day

Dear Diary,

This morning was the first morning I woke up next to Ethan in a long time. We finally get to sleep together again after our break, we had. It took all of yesterday for Malinda and her father to pack up and leave back home to Georgia. Justin was frustrated with all of us, but we all knew to live with it. Once again, we had to rearrange how the rooms are because mama was going to live with us. I'm so happy to have my mama with me after all we both have gone through. I'm pleased to have Elizabeth and Eric as good friends and family and also Molly as my soon to be mother in law.

Earlier in the day, the family would be sitting in the family room laughing and talking. I'm happy to have Ethan as my love and soon to be husband someday in the future. This day has been a really good day for me. Justin how ever has been mad all day so he just keeps to himself for now. Ethan and I sit side by side at the table holding hands under it secretly. We would glance over to each other and start laughing. At this moment, I know that *love comes through time.*

Love Katherine

About the Author

I'm a first time book writer who has the passion to be a writer.

I've started this as a hobby and turned it into a career choice in publishing books.

I am born and raised in Greenfield, Indiana, I would like to live on a rural ranch or farm to continue writing additional books.

Printed in the United States
By Bookmasters